'Hello, Rach[...] deep, smoot[...] accented nov[...] same mesmeric quality. 'How are you?'

He hadn't expected this—that she should look virtually the same. Here she was, six years older, and she was still as fresh and young and as beautiful as ever...

Rachel forced her gaze away from Jean-Luc's face, stared at his strong, tanned fingers for a moment in a daze. 'I'm...fine,' she murmured automatically. 'Just fine...'

He wondered if he would be able to keep this up—to act as if the sight of her had little or no effect on him. He was a man who supposedly thrived on challenge, but this was a bigger challenge than any he had ever attempted— except maybe the one of trying to forget her...

Laura Martin lives in a small Gloucestershire village with her husband, two young children and a lively sheepdog! Laura has a great love of interior design and, together with her husband, has recently completed the renovation of their Victorian cottage. Her hobbies include gardening, the theatre, music and reading, and she finds great pleasure and inspiration from walking daily in the beautiful countryside around her home.

Recent titles by the same author:

LIVING WITH THE ENEMY
FALLING FOR THE BOSS

HIS PERFECT PARTNER

BY
LAURA MARTIN

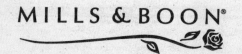

MILLS & BOON®

*First published in Great Britain 1998
Harlequin Mills & Boon Limited,
Eton House, 18-24 Paradise Road, Richmond, Surrey TW9 1SR*

© Laura Martin 1998

ISBN 0 263 81151 4

*Set in Times Roman 10½ on 11 pt.
02-9809-53206 C1*

*Printed and bound in Norway
by AiT Trondheim AS, Trondheim*

CHAPTER ONE

JEAN-LUC MANOIRE frowned. He wasn't entirely sure that he was doing the right thing. Indecision and compulsion were unhappy bedfellows, and neither was a state of mind that he was at all comfortable with.

Too late now. They were here. He leant forward and touched his chauffeur on the shoulder, indicating that he wanted the car to slow.

Jean-Luc stared up at the tall iron gates. They told the story as well as any inanimate object ever could—rusty, they hung awkwardly from the crumbling stone wall that surrounded the estate. He inhaled a deep breath, more conscious than ever of the conflicting emotions which were churning around deep inside. '*D'accord, Emile. Continuez!*'

The car glided forward, the tyres crunching on gravel. The trees that lined the drive were just coming into bud. Lime, he remembered, looking up at the tall, statuesque framework of branches, at least one hundred years old.

The house looked empty and neglected. He hoped the enquiries he had made proved to be reliable. Time was money, and driving this far out of London on such a tightly scheduled trip, only to find her not at home, would be aggravating to say the least.

His mobile phone rang and he retrieved it from the briefcase at his side and took the call he had been expecting. He spoke into it, his comments brief and to the point as he listened to his personal assistant many miles away in Paris, confirming the fact that the final transaction on an important business deal had been completed without a hitch.

Business. That was all he had to focus on—just business. The rest...the other, more complex reasons for his involvement here had to be put to one side, or else how would he cope? He still doubted his ability to act with absolute composure. He had been dwelling on this meeting for days—ever since the situation here had first come to his attention.

A death notice in the English papers, that was all it had taken. Thoughts of her, banished for so long, had haunted him day and night. He couldn't sleep, he could barely eat, business had lost its attraction.

Except for this deal... She would agree to it. The generosity of his offer made financial sense. Her advisers would practically force her to accept.

And if they didn't?

She would have changed—he had prepared himself for that, counted on it. Because if she were the same how would he ever be able to get through... ?

Arrêtez! How Rachel looked after all these years, her reaction on seeing him again—none of that could be dwelt on. He needed to be in control. He *was* over her—this was just an exercise to confirm as much. Devastation was a strong word, and it had applied to him, but that had been six years ago.

Jean-Luc cursed silently as a vision of Rachel, lying beneath him, golden hair splayed out, eyes wide with trust and love, jolted into his mind—that days later she could have disregarded what they had had together and walked away from him, from his love...

Just business. He must remember that.

'Here you are! I wondered where you'd got to.'

Rachel turned sharply at the sound of the elderly woman's voice. She watched as Naomi approached, forcing a smile. 'How did you know I was here?'

'I spotted you from one of the upstairs windows.'

Naomi folded her arms across her ample chest and sighed. 'Your Aunt Clara was a hoarder and no mistake—there's still a ton of junk to clear out up there.'

'Yes, I should be doing something.' Rachel rose to her feet. 'Sorry, Naomi, I didn't mean to leave you alone for so long. I just needed a breath of fresh air.'

'Now don't be silly, my girl, I'm not complaining. You needed the break. It's been a week since your dear aunt's funeral and you haven't let up for a minute.' The old woman placed a sympathetic arm around Rachel's shoulders and squeezed gently. 'I've come to find you because you have a visitor.'

'Not another creditor?' Rachel asked wearily. 'I thought we'd had our fill of those.'

'And so did I, but these things are best faced. He gave me this card.' She held out a gilt-edged business card to Rachel. 'From some corporation or some such,' she added. 'I'd tell you what it says, but I'm blind without my reading glasses. Important, though—if the look of him and his car are anything to go by. Wealthy,' she added, with an approving nod.

Rachel shrugged as she read the name. 'JSJ Corporation. Means nothing to me, but, then...' she sighed '...neither did the hundred and one other names that were thrust under my nose by the accountant.' She stood up, stretching her arms high above her head. 'OK, let's go back. I may as well see what this man wants and get it over with. Tomorrow is crunch day, anyway. I have to face the bank manager to discover exactly how deep the estate is in trouble, and decide—or rather be told—what has to be done.'

'These are difficult times, my dear. If only I'd understood what was going on maybe you wouldn't be in this mess.'

'It's not your fault.' Rachel's voice was kind. 'You mustn't blame yourself. Aunt Clara was...' Rachel smiled. 'Well, she was what she was—a strong-willed woman. She wouldn't have been advised by anyone. When she decided on a course of action she stuck to her guns, no matter what anyone else said or did. There's nothing any of us could have done, even if we had realised what was going on. You know that as well as I do.'

'Yes…' Naomi's already creased forehead became even more lined. 'That is *so* true.' The old woman was silent for a moment, then she added in more upbeat tones, 'Shaun phoned again—did I tell you?'

'Yes.' Rachel heaved a breath. 'Yes, you did. Naomi…it is over between us. I know you're fond of him, but—'

'But the two of you are perfect for each other! I believe it, and I know Shaun does, too.'

'No.' Rachel shook her head. 'Naomi, I don't want to disappoint you because I know Shaun's your nephew—'

'Great-nephew,' Naomi corrected. 'His mother is my sister's daughter.'

'He's a relation,' Rachel continued. 'I like him, I like him a lot, but…it just wasn't working out between us.'

'You need someone.' Naomi's voice was firm. 'Like Shaun.'

Rachel didn't bother to argue any further. In many respects Naomi was like her Aunt Clara had been—stubborn, sure of her own point of view. Indeed, the two woman had virtually grown up together, albeit one as the mistress and the other as the maid.

They walked in silence towards the back of the house, both women, so varied in age and appearance, deep in their own thoughts.

'I've shown him into the drawing room,' Naomi announced, as they reached the kitchen door. 'Do you want to spruce yourself up a bit before you go in?'

Rachel paused, glancing at her reflection in the pantry window. Her long blonde hair was shiny and clean, if a little ruffled. She lifted her hands and resecured the ribbon, which was hanging loosely down her back. 'I don't look that bad, do I?' she asked.

'Your clothes aren't very smart,' Naomi informed her with her customary bluntness. 'It's as well to give a good impression.'

Rachel looked down at her clean, if rather tatty denims and comfortable violet jumper. 'Oh, well, it can't be helped,' she replied. 'I don't suppose my appearance will make much of a difference to things. Besides, it's not worth changing. I want to get back and continue going through Aunt Clara's things afterwards.' Rachel threw Naomi a self-deprecating smile.

'I'm still foolishly hoping that I'll discover some hidden treasure that will get us out of this financial nightmare—a forgotten Constable, or a rare first edition, something of that sort.'

'From what I've seen you've got as much chance of that as of me winning the lottery!' Naomi announced with a snort.

'But you never buy a ticket for the lottery,' Rachel replied, her thoughts elsewhere, most particularly with the ordeal of having to face another creditor.

Naomi's face curved into a grim smile. 'Exactly!' she retorted.

Rachel paused, before entering the drawing room. She felt *so* tired. Nothing could have prepared her for the shock of the last few days. Her aunt's sudden death had been bad enough, but to discover that her finances were in the mess they were had only served to drag Rachel's emotions down further.

Still, she was determined to get through this one way or another—to see the whole sorry episode through to the end. She felt it was her keen duty to do all she could to protect the Grange as far as was humanly possible. It had been in her family for generations, and although she took it for granted, hating the miles of draughty corridors and high-ceilinged rooms, she didn't want to see it lost to the bank.

Sonia, one of the women from the village who had been working at the Grange for as long as Rachel could remember, smiled sympathetically at her as she descended the stairway, carrying yet another sackful of rubbish from her Aunt Clara's chambers. 'Looking better up there,' she commented. 'You'll soon have this all sorted out, don't you worry.'

Rachel returned her smile, preparing to open the drawing-room door, and wished she shared the woman's confidence.

'Sorry to have kept you,' she began briskly, as she walked into the drawing room. 'Only, as you can imagine, it's a bit hectic around here at the moment.'

The man, who was standing at the far end of the room before the fireplace, turned as she spoke, and the first stab of recognition felt like a knife, twisting deep in her stomach.

Rachel stared, her blue eyes wide with shocked surprise. She clutched her chest involuntarily as a kind of protection for her heart, which had jolted painfully at the first sight of him and was now pounding away like a steam engine out of control. She shook her head, a slow, disbelieving movement that felt as strange and as awkward as the situation that now presented itself.

It was... No. *No!* She forgot to breathe. Yes, *yes*! It *was* him. Her mind wasn't playing tricks on her; grief and stress and a too-vivid imagination hadn't made her lose her sense. He was here, in this bright, sunny drawing room with its faded chintz and eclectic assortment of flowers and books and china ornaments, looking even more out of place than he had done all those years ago.

Rachel stared at the dark, silky hair, tamed and cut now into a short, almost severe style, at the strong jaw and finely moulded mouth, and felt a wave of dizziness overcome her. *Jean-Luc!* She reached out trembling hands and gripped the back of a nearby chair for support.

'Hello, Rachel.' His voice was deep, smooth—not so heavily accented now, but still with the same mesmeric quality. 'How are you?'

He hesitated for a moment, then crossed the room towards her, holding out his hand in formal greeting—as if, she thought, to greet her thus was the most natural thing in the world.

He hadn't expected this—that she should look virtually the same. He had learned of her rise up the career ladder, and had convinced himself that she would look altogether more sophisticated, more a woman of the world, more, in fact, like many of the women he now dated. But she didn't. Here she was, six years older, and she was still as fresh and young and as beautiful as ever...

Rachel forced her gaze away from Jean-Luc's face, stared at his strong, tanned fingers for a moment in a daze and then found herself shaking his hand. 'I'm...fine,' she murmured automatically. 'Just fine...'

'I've come at a difficult time.'

'Yes.' She couldn't think straight, hardly knew *what* to think. He looked older, more sensationally attractive, if that were possible, but different. Sharper, groomed, more...polished and refined, not like the Jean-Luc Manoire she had known and loved. Not at all.

'I was sorry to hear about the death of your aunt.'

'Were you?' Now that the horrendous initial shock was over, Rachel could begin to think a little more clearly. 'I don't see why,' she added stiltedly. 'You always disliked her.'

'And that translates to wanting to see her dead, does it?' His voice was mild, but there was the hint of steel at the edge of each perfectly spoken syllable.

Rachel released a taut breath. It had been a foolish remark, born out of shock and sheer nervousness. He wasn't the sort of man you could treat casually—she should have remembered that.

She glanced down at the faded carpet, desperately trying to compose herself, and said, 'No, of course it doesn't.'

'You sound weary. You look—'

'I know how I look!' Rachel's voice was tinged with anger. She pursed her lips, determined to save him the trouble of lying. 'I look a mess!' She cleared her throat, conscious of her trembling voice. She usually looked immaculate—her position as manager of a small prestigious hotel in the Cotswolds demanded it. Typical, she thought, that he should see me this way—so ragged and ill at ease.

'Let's forget the formalities, shall we?' she continued. 'I think I'd just prefer it if you told me what it is you're doing here!'

Her words set the tone. She watched his expression. Not a flicker of expression marked Jean-Luc's angular face—just the slightest tightening of the jaw, maybe a hardening of the ebony eyes. He knew how she felt, how she wanted things to be, how things *had* to be.

'Very little has changed here,' Jean-Luc commented, glancing around the room that looked as if it had been locked in a time warp for the past fifty years. His dark eyes came to rest on Rachel's pale face. 'Except maybe you.'

'I'm older!' she responded flatly. But not wiser, she thought despondently, aware of the agony of her thudding heart. Definitely not that.

'And poorer, I understand.' Jean-Luc's glance was cool, controlled. Almost cruel in its ability to calmly survey her face.

He wondered if he would be able to keep this up—to act as if the sight of her had little or no effect on him. He was a man who supposedly thrived on challenge, but this was a bigger challenge than any he had ever attempted—except maybe the one of trying to forget her, of course.

Rachel met the uncaring gaze with a cold expression, marvelling in some far-off corner of her mind at her capacity to even begin to cope with this conversation. 'Yes, quite poor.' Her voice was like ice.

'A shock, I should think,' Jean-Luc continued. 'Your aunt always gave such a good impression of being a wealthy woman.'

'She *was* a wealthy woman,' Rachel responded swiftly. 'She just made some wrong choices, invested badly…' Her voice trailed away. 'Am I to presume, then, that you've come all the way here to offer your condolences?' she asked, after a slight but telling pause. 'You're a little late. The funeral was early last week and, as you can undoubtedly see,' she added, glancing at the muddled room, 'I am still in the middle of sorting through and clearing everything out. So, if you'll excuse me—'

'You misunderstand, Rachel,' Jean-Luc replied crisply, forestalling her retreat towards the door. 'This isn't a *social* call.'

'No?'

'Naomi gave you my card, I presume?'

Rachel had almost forgotten about it. She thrust a hand into the pocket of her jeans and retrieved it. 'She did.' She hesitated a moment then walked on slightly unsteady legs over to a side table, where a selection of bottles and glasses stood on a tray. She poured herself a measure of mineral water and took a healthy gulp— her mouth was so dry she could hardly talk any more.

'Not that it meant anything to me—JSJ Corporation?' She glanced at the card in her hand, raising arched eyebrows—trying to play it cool. 'Another faceless conglomerate—is that who you work for?'

'In a manner of speaking.' Jean-Luc strolled over to stand beside her. 'May I?' he asked, and began pouring a small measure of whisky into a tumbler before Rachel could say a thing. 'I'm surprised you haven't heard of it. JSJ has its fingers in several very large pies.' He reeled off a handful of well-known projects that had received recent media attention in countries worldwide, and Rachel finally had to admit defeat and acknowledge with a slight nod that she had heard of at least some of them.

'OK! OK! I get the picture. JSJ is a legitimate firm.' She moved away—because to stand so close to Jean-Luc after all these years was torture of the worst kind— and walked over to the window to look out through the leaded panes at the car parked on the weedy, gravelled drive.

It was large and swish and very expensive. It matched this new image of Jean-Luc, the one that Rachel was having such difficulty coming to terms with—immaculate, powerful, an uncompromising presence that made heads turn and would not, or could not, be ignored.

He had clearly done very well for himself. Rachel had imagined her success in the hotel trade as being pretty impressive, considering she had started on one of the bottom rungs of the ladder as a lowly part-time receptionist and had worked her way up with determination and not a small amount of natural flair, but it was clear that her achievements were nowhere near on the same scale as this.

A chauffeur-driven car meant status, and that equalled success far beyond anything she had ever, or would ever, manage to achieve.

She spun around and said, 'Forgive me for being dense, but I still don't see what a company like the JSJ Corporation would find of interest here—a run-down country estate like this. Is your boss totally mad?'

'I'm beginning to think so.' She turned then to look at Jean-Luc. There had been something in his voice...

'The initials of the company—they obviously don't mean a great deal to you,' he added briskly.

'No.' Rachel lifted her shoulders in an uncaring shrug, turned back toward the window and closed her eyes tightly against shared memories which were bombarding her senses. 'Why on earth should they?'

Jean-Luc, Saul, Jerome—an excessive number of names, I always thought, but, then, my mother and father did only manage to have one child.'

'JSJ...?' It took a moment for Rachel to realise the significance of what he was saying. '*Your* company?' she added in disbelieving tones. No matter how hard she tried, Rachel couldn't hide the astonishment in her voice. She looked at this new, sharp, hard Jean-Luc—so different from the man she had worshipped, loved—and tried to reconcile the differences between now and six years ago. 'You mean you actually own...?'

Her voice trailed away in shocked disbelief as she stood and stared and tried to come to terms with the fact that Jean-Luc, the student, had transformed himself into a business magnate of quite incredible proportions.

'Six years is a long time,' he drawled smoothly. 'What did you expect? That time should have stood still? That I would still be tending other people's gardens?'

'No, of course not!' Rachel's voice was hard. 'But it's not that long ago either...' She made up her mind, and walked towards the door on legs that felt like jelly. 'Would you please leave?' She wondered if he could see the glistening of tears in her eyes from this distance, and decided that he probably couldn't. 'I don't think we have a great deal to say to one another!'

'So polite, Miss Shaw.' Jean-Luc's voice was deliberately heavy with mockery. 'I see those beautiful English manners that I remember so well haven't entirely deserted you.'

'I don't want to talk to you!' Rachel's restraint was

slowly beginning to give way. 'I don't see what possible
reason you have for coming here.'

'This estate is deeply in debt. You are in very real
danger of losing everything. That is correct, isn't it?' His
crisp tones cut through the atmosphere which lay heavy
between them.

'How clever you are!' Rachel retorted harshly. 'So my
financial position is common knowledge, then?'

'No, it is not. I have just made it my business to find
out what is happening here, that's all.'

'Oh, really! And why is that?' Rachel asked frostily.
'Am I supposed to feel flattered you've taken such an
interest?'

'*Flattered?*' He made her suffer by pretending to be
dense, and threw Rachel a look of puzzlement that made
her want to curl up and die right in front of him, making
him almost hate himself. 'I do not think flattery enters
the equation. Oh, I see,' he added cruelly, 'you maybe
imagined that I had kept some sort of a tab on the place
because of old associations?' There was a cutting smile,
the flash of even, white teeth. 'Sentimentality.' He
arched a dark brow. 'Never my forte.'

Rachel placed a hand to her brow. She was having
trouble coping with all of this. It was bad enough that
she should be losing her home, but even worse to have
Jean-Luc by her side, pointing out the awful fact.
'So...what do you want?' she asked unsteadily, eyeing
him with obvious dislike.

'I can help.'

Rachel looked into the enigmatic dark eyes. 'Help
me? Are you *crazy*?' She inhaled, trying to keep her
voice as steady as possible. 'Do you honestly believe
that I would want any help of yours?'

'Whether you *want* it or not—that is immaterial,' he
replied coolly. 'You need it. You have found debts every
which way you turn because of your aunt's inability to

take financial advice, and tomorrow the bank will fore-close. Isn't that correct?'

'I…I have some money of my own,' Rachel informed him unsteadily. 'I'm not wildly rich, but I have some resources to call upon.'

'Enough to retrieve this place from the impatient hands of the bank?' Jean-Luc shook his head. 'Stop fooling yourself! You might have scrimped and saved every penny for the past few years, but it would be chicken feed compared to what would be needed to get yourself out of debt and pay for the upkeep of such a large estate.' He crossed the room towards her, standing close.

'Are you prepared to lose this place just because you're too stubborn to listen to what I have to say?' His tone was harsh and full of derision. 'I can't believe you'd be that foolish.'

'Believe what you like!' Rachel replied shakily. 'After all, I was foolish enough all those years ago to allow a smooth-talking Frenchman to get me into his bed!'

Silence. The room seemed still suddenly—even the clock on the mantelpiece seemed to suspend its ticking.

'As I recall, we first made love on the grass,' Jean-Luc replied quietly.

'How dare you?' Rachel continued shakily. 'How dare you march in here, telling me that I must listen to you? Just who do you think you are?'

'I know what I was.'

Rachel gasped as Jean-Luc snaked out a hand to prevent her from flouncing off towards the door. He pulled her close and suddenly it was like six years ago as he looked down into her trembling face, except that this time there was an element of punishment and force in his expression, along with the compelling tension and the supreme sexual vitality which was so much a part of him. 'This place means something to you. Don't be a fool and allow old prejudices to cloud your judgement just because we were once—'

'Let me go!' Rachel struggled free. She didn't need to be reminded what they had once been to each other. Every nerve end in her body tingled with recollection—with a dreadful and intolerable yearning that had sparked into life the moment she had set eyes on him. 'You think you can return after all these years and presume to tell me about the way I feel!' she retorted angrily. 'You, of all people!'

'I don't presume—I know,' Jean-Luc informed her with disconcerting arrogance. So this was how it was going to be, he told himself—acrimonious, bitter. And to think that he had once been fool enough to imagine she'd loved him as much as he'd loved her.

'Now.' He kept his voice hard. 'I have come here with a genuine business proposition. Are you prepared to stop acting like a petulant little girl and listen, or do you want to lose everything?' Dark brows were raised questioningly. 'Think carefully, Rachel, which is it to be?'

CHAPTER TWO

RACHEL wanted to run away. She wanted to scream and cry with anger and frustration—yell at Jean-Luc who was nothing but a cold-hearted, unfeeling swine. He had devastated her life. How dared he come back and open up all the old wounds? How dared he speak to her this way? How dared he?

But she didn't move. Instinct told her that he would surely get the better of any scene she chose to make, just as before, just as always. And, besides, to display the way she felt would be to indicate that everything mattered—that *he* mattered—and that was the last thing she wanted.

'OK.' Rachel inhaled a steadying breath. 'Say what you've got to say.'

'Not here.' He dismissed her offer without the slightest hesitation, pulling back his cuff to glance at the watch on his wrist. 'Not now. I'm already late for another appointment. It will have to be later.'

'How much later?' Rachel struggled to keep the fury out of her voice. 'I haven't got that much time. I have an appointment with the trustees of Aunt Clara's estate and the bank manager first thing in the morning.'

'We'll talk this evening—over dinner.' Jean-Luc surveyed her with a cool expression. 'Then I will arrange for my accountant and solicitor to meet with your financial advisers so that things can move as swiftly as possible. My car will pick you up at eight.'

'What if I don't want to have dinner with you?'

Dark eyes scanned Rachel's flushed face. 'It's part of the deal—besides, that is the only time that I have free.'

'My, my! What a busy person you are!' Sarcasm hardened Rachel's voice, and she turned away towards the
window.

'Eight o'clock.' Jean-Luc's voice was brisk and
businesslike. There was a slight pause. Rachel had to
summon all her will-power not to turn and look at him
at the sound of the drawing-room door being opened.
'*Au revoir.*'

Rachel watched through the window as he walked to
his car, her eyes drawn by every inch of his smartly
suited figure. A chauffeur opened a rear door and Jean-
Luc climbed inside. There must have been a briefcase
on the rear seat for she saw him lift a black leather object
onto his lap, open it and draw out a sheaf of papers. He
was working.

Was it really as easy as that for him? No time for
reflection? Rachel wondered. No need to dwell on the
fact that he had seen her again after all this time?
Evidently not.

He was shaking. Jean-Luc stared at his trembling hand
and gripped the business report he was holding a little
tighter. What had he expected? What, exactly? That she
would be pleased to see him? That she might care that
he had put aside the pain of the past in order to help her
when she needed it most?

He looked up and saw that Emile was watching him
in the rear-view mirror. What would he be making of
this? His employer, usually so cool and calculating, so
in control.

Jean-Luc inhaled a calming breath and released it with
a vow that he would not allow memories of the past to
interfere with the here and now. Foolishly, he hadn't
expected to feel this way, so…disturbed by her. He pic-
tured again the hate in her eyes. Her dismay at seeing
him again had been clear.

The car swung away from the Grange and he caught
sight of her at the window, watching him. Blonde and

beautiful. How many hours had he spent, convincing himself that he was over her, before he'd decided on this course of action? Jean-Luc's mouth firmed into a formidable line. Too many.

Rachel didn't move for a long while, even when the vehicle was just a dark speck in the distance and the only evidence that he had been with her was the faint scent of his cologne and the thudding of her heart.

She could scarcely believe that he had been here, that she would have to endure the torture of seeing him again. Rachel held her head in her hands and sobbed as if her heart would break.

Naomi found her some ten minutes later. The old woman bustled into the room, a frown of concern creasing an already lined face. 'My dear, whatever is it? What's wrong?'

'Everything!' Rachel's voice broke with emotion. 'Everything,' she repeated, picturing the scenes she had had to endure with Jean-Luc.

'There! There! You have a good cry. I don't think I've seen you shed a tear since your poor Aunt Clara's funeral. It's not good for you to keep all that emotion locked away inside. I know you miss her.' Naomi paused to administer comfort in the form of a plump arm around Rachel's shoulders. 'Where's your visitor?'

'He's left.'

'Wasn't here long.' She handed Rachel a wad of clean tissues. 'These tears aren't anything to do with him, are they?' she asked suspiciously. 'You should have called me. I would have given him a piece of my mind, and him looking so nice and respectable, too. Hounding you for money, was he?'

'Not exactly.' Rachel wiped her eyes, struggling for composure. 'He's got a…a business proposition he wants to put to me,' she croaked. 'I'm meeting him again this evening… He's picking me up at eight.'

'You're going out with him?' Naomi sounded horrified. 'But you can't do that—you don't know him from Adam!'

Rachel glanced at Naomi and saw from her expression that she really didn't have a clue as to the identity of the suave and sophisticated gentleman she had shown into the drawing room. If only she knew! Rachel didn't want to tell her, not at this moment, anyway, not while she herself was feeling so shell-shocked. 'He comes from a reputable company,' she murmured. 'It will be...all right.'

'Well, I hope so. A business proposition, you say?' Naomi's voice brightened. 'Might there be chance of saving the Grange, then?' she added hopefully.

'I'm not sure.' Rachel struggled to bring her tears under control, but a sob caught in her throat. 'But if there's a chance, I suppose I must try...'

She couldn't decide what to wear—not that it mattered one iota, of course. It was a toss-up between making every effort and making no effort at all. In the end Rachel decided that pride had to show its more attractive face, and she chose a simple, yet elegant long-sleeved dress in fine black wool from her wardrobe.

His car was on time. Rachel, pacing nervously in the hallway, almost jumped out of her skin when the doorbell clanged. She was nervous—more than that, petrified. Jean-Luc's unexpected appearance earlier that afternoon had had a debilitating effect. She hadn't been able to do a thing in the intervening hours since his visit. She'd just sat and thought and remembered how it had been during those last glorious few days...

'Wake up, sleepyhead!'

Rachel stirred faintly as the sensuous voice penetrated her dreams. She moved in the bed, hugging the crisp, white linen sheets close around her slender body, and smiled dreamily.

'Do you always look this gorgeous in the morning?' Jean-Luc's deep voice, heavy with the seductive French accent was soft and enticing against her lips. 'Baby, come on,' he whispered, 'open those beautiful blue eyes.'

She raised dark lashes and looked up in sleepy astonishment at the rugged, handsome face, lifting a hand in something approaching wonderment to touch the angled cheekbone. 'Jean-Luc?' Rachel smiled lovingly, hardly able to believe he was here with her. 'What are you doing?'

He didn't allow her to finish the sentence, not that she cared. His lips moved with possessive intent over her mouth, and Rachel found herself responding, despite the early hour and the fact that she was still half-asleep, despite the awful possibility that he could be found here in her bedroom by one of the servants or, worse still, her Aunt Clara at any moment.

She entwined her hands around his strong, suntanned neck and accepted his kiss, revelling in the strength and the warmth of his body—wondering once again how she had ever survived without it, ever survived without *him*.

Jean-Luc was so brave, so bold, so totally alien, like a wonderful being from another planet, entering her co-cooned world, changing her perspective on life.

'Hurry, *ma chérie*! It's a beautiful day and I don't want us to waste a second of it!' He kissed her mouth lovingly once again, then disentangled her arms and pulled back the bedclothes, a smile curving his mouth at the sight of Rachel's extremely functional cotton pyjamas.

'Well, it's cold in the country!' She glanced down at her attire, wishing she looked more seductive for him, and pulled a comical face to hide her embarrassment. 'My bedroom doesn't have central heating.'

'Don't worry, you look beautiful.' Jean-Luc ran a fingertip along the line of pearl buttons, tormenting her with the lightness of his touch. His dark eyes sparkled. 'Fresh and sweet as the daisy.'

Rachel pouted. 'Not even a little sophisticated and alluring?'

He pulled her to him and kissed her mouth. 'Sophisticated—no. Alluring—definitely. 'You are the sweetest of temptations.' He looked at her as she had never seen him look at her before—naked desire in his eyes, the hunger of wanting her, pure rugged masculinity in every taut line, every fleeting expression. '*Mon Dieu*!' The words were a groan beneath his breath. 'How to resist you?'

'Don't try.' Rachel's eyes were wide and bold. She had never felt this way about any man before, knew with a deeply felt certainty that she never would again. 'You know how I feel about you.'

'For me it is the same.' He tugged her into the circle of his arms to kiss her again with a passion that took all her breath away. 'Always,' he asserted huskily, drawing back a little to look deep into her eyes. 'For ever.'

'You mean that?' Rachel's voice was barely a whisper.

'Of course.' He kissed her again. Rachel loved the wonderful fact that she seemed to be irresistible to him. It was quiet in the bedroom for several minutes. Rachel knew she would never forget this moment. Jean-Luc's gaze, his tender hands, told her all she needed to know. He loved her, just as she loved him.

Never mind what Aunt Clara thought, it wasn't her fault. She was just…old, out of touch, unaware of the depth of feeling between them. Once she understood the seriousness of their relationship, Rachel told herself, everything would be better. She would be happy for her niece, happy that she had found love.

'You're frowning.' Jean-Luc's dark brows drew together in comical imitation of hers, his smile gently teasing. 'Have I woken you too early? Would you prefer to be a lazybones and sleep in?' He lifted her into his arms suddenly and laid her back down on the bed. 'Would you like to stay here?' he murmured huskily, kissing her neck. 'Shall we both stay here?'

'You know we can't.' Rachel linked her arms around Jean-Luc's neck. 'If Aunt Clara or Naomi finds you here...' She glanced towards the closed door of her bedroom, conscious of the sounds of the house below. 'How on earth did you get up here, anyway?' she asked, smiling. 'And don't tell me you knocked on the front door, informed Hayes that you wished to see me and simply marched straight upstairs to my bedroom because I won't believe you!'

'Do I look that mad?' Jean-Luc replied, with a curl of a smile. 'No, I did the correct thing and took the tradesman's entrance.'

'But surely Naomi was busy in the kitchen?'

'She was. But I have a very good line in distraction.' Jean-Luc's eyes sparkled mischievously. 'I knocked at the kitchen door, hid around the side of the house, Naomi came out, followed my trail and...' He gestured with his hands. '*Voilà!* I simply slipped inside.'

'Trail?' Rachel's expression was a mixture of perplexity and excitement. 'What do you mean?'

'The milkman had been. There were eggs, a lot of them. I simply placed them in a line which led away from the house. Naomi followed like *un canard*...a duck, waddling after a trail of bread!'

'You are incorrigible!' Rachel smiled happily, kissing his mouth. 'You do know that, don't you?'

'*Incorrigible?*' Jean-Luc's sensuous eyes gleamed. 'What is that?'

'Naughty!' Rachel kissed his finely moulded mouth. 'Very naughty indeed!'

'I like naughty.' Jean-Luc cradled Rachel's blonde

head with both hands and returned her kiss. 'It feels good. Now, come!' He rolled away from her suddenly, and Rachel knew that he was having to exert the utmost will-power as he rose from the bed. 'Get dressed. It's a beautiful morning—the sun is shining, the birds are singing. I want us to share every second of it together.'

Rachel did as he requested. It never entered her head to refuse—why should it? This was what she wanted—this excitement, this sense of freedom and fun. This passion.

Jean-Luc lifted the sash window while Rachel slipped on jeans and a jumper. She watched him as he stood with his back to her, breathing in the fresh spring air. She loved to look at him. Her blue eyes lingered on the broad shoulders, on the dark brown, slightly wavy hair that brushed the collar of his blue linen shirt, on the clean, but undeniably worn denims that hugged slim hips.

He was everything she'd ever wanted. It really was as simple as that. *Everything.* The fluttering sensations of desire and excitement had been old friends ever since that day almost two months ago when he had first come to work in the gardens for her aunt.

'Ready?' He turned, holding out a hand, leading her towards the window. 'We are taking an alternative route.' His lips curved at Rachel's expression. 'Don't look so shocked. It will be perfectly safe. See? We step out onto the flat roof, then a careful negotiation of the drainpipes and a small leap down to freedom.'

Rachel smiled. 'Maybe you should have rung the front doorbell,' she said, stretching up on tiptoe and kissing him tenderly. 'I think it would have been a lot simpler.'

'Ah, but not so much fun. And, besides,' he continued, with more than a hint of bitterness, 'I would have had to wait until much later in the day, and then I would have had to endure the disapproving looks of your aunt—it really isn't the done thing for the gardener's boy to court the mistress's niece, is it?'

'Don't, Jean-Luc, please, not now!' Rachel placed a fingertip to the suddenly angry mouth, hating the old argument coming between them once again. 'Aunt Clara's just being protective. I'm just eighteen. I'm the only family she's got. She only wants to look after me—'

'To stifle you.' Angry brown eyes held Rachel's gaze. 'She imagines I would hurt you?' The incredulity in Jean-Luc's tone was hard to miss. He shook his head in disgust. 'I swear, this house, it is still living in the Victorian times. Your aunt would look very convincing in a black gown with a white lace cap on her head!' His mouth curved, but beneath the humour the anger was still evident.

'She doesn't trust me because I'm a foreigner...or a gardener...' He lifted his hands in a typically Gallic gesture. 'What does she think I'm going to do—whisk you off and sell you to the white slave trade?'

'Jean-Luc!' Rachel shook her head. 'Please! Don't be cross.' Rachel glanced anxiously towards her bedroom door again.

'Although, I think,' he added, pulling her close against his rugged body, his smouldering eyes lingering over Rachel's feminine curves, 'it might not be such a bad idea. I think you would fetch a very good price.'

Rachel giggled. 'Jean-Luc, you are not only incorrigible, you are irreverent, too!' She stood on tiptoe and kissed his mouth. 'Do you think that's why I like you so *very* much?'

'*Like?*' He pulled her closer still so that she felt the full power of his body against hers, and tipped her face back so that her long golden hair fell free behind her like a waterfall of pure gossamer. 'What is "like"?' he growled in mock anger....

Rachel negotiated the climb down over the rooftops,

laughing because she had never felt so carefree, so incredibly happy. In a few short weeks Jean-Luc had become everything to her—the sun, the moon, the stars. She would follow him to the ends of the earth if he asked her, walk on a bed of hot coals if it meant spending the rest of her life with him.

In comparison to all of that, a short trip over the rooftops was nothing.

They ran like the wind, hand in hand, around the side of the huge manor house, across the crunching gravel drive and out through the wooden door in the walled kitchen garden into the fields beyond...

Rachel hardly noticed the outside world. Her only thoughts were for Jean-Luc. Uncaring of her aunt's disapproval, every spare moment was spent with him. Early morning rendezvous became the norm. Beautiful hours spent walking and talking, passionate encounters in orchard or barn—anywhere. It didn't matter, as long as they could be together.

Rachel had never imagined that such happiness as she felt could exist. During the beauty of those few precious weeks together the whole world was transformed into a glorious place. She loved Jean-Luc with all her innocent heart and told him so a thousand times, never imagining that his declarations of love in their most passionate of moments meant as much as his promise that he would stay with her for ever.

In the days that followed Jean-Luc's departure Rachel tried hard to keep faith, to hope that he would be missing her as much as she was missing him and that he would come back simply because he loved her.

The doubts crept in, of course. Once so sure of what they had together, Rachel began to look at aspects of their time together and understood that what had been for her the most important relationship of her life had been for Jean-Luc simply a passionate holiday romance.

The shock of discovering he was gone, after returning

from a weekend visit to a friend, had been profound, to say the least. On that Friday afternoon she had kissed him goodbye without a care in the world, confident that he would be at the Grange, working still and waiting for her on Monday morning. So sure of what they had to-gether—*too* sure.

At first she refused to believe he'd gone. His letter had clinched it, of course, propped up on her cluttered dressing-table when she had returned… Rachel inhaled a ragged breath. Even now, she could scarcely bring her-self to think of it. The letter had been so kind—too kind almost, stilted and strange. The agonies of having to tell her that he didn't want to see her again, she supposed. Whatever, it had given out little hope.

In some ways it was the kindness, the altered, distant tone of Jean-Luc's missive, that had hurt Rachel the most. She hadn't wanted to read about how much their romance had meant to him, how intensely he valued the time they had shared together, that he would remember it always, think of her often. Platitudes, that's all they had been—empty platitudes.

She wanted him to be there with her—for always.

She thought hard about trying to contact him and was dismayed when she realised that, apart from the region, she knew little about where he came from and who he really was. She had been so wrapped up in each moment, in the precious time they had shared together. When she thought back, Rachel realised that he had been peculiarly reticent about discussing his family, his life in France. Sure, he had talked about the beauty and his love of his country, but very little of it had been detailed or precise. Only when Jean-Luc had gone did she understand why.

It was difficult, coping with her heartbreak alone—impossible, in fact. Aunt Clara was surprisingly sym-pathetic when a sobbing Rachel confessed why she was in such an appalling state.

'My dear, I don't want to say I told you so, but you

know I really wasn't happy about the amount of time you were spending with each other. Did you really believe,' she added gently, 'that there could be a future with a man like that?'

'A man like that?' Rachel pulled away from her embrace, still keen to defend Jean-Luc, despite everything. 'What do you mean?'

'Silly, silly girl! He's young—only a couple of years older than yourself—virile, full of his own ambitions. You didn't honestly think that there was a future for the two of you?'

'Yes!' Rachel's expression revealed her anguish. 'Yes!' she repeated, the word strangled by a sob. 'I did.'

Her aunt suggested getting away, and offered to pay for a long-wanted trip to America to visit distant relations. Rachel, although reluctant in the first few days following Jean-Luc's departure, soon saw the advantages of such a decision. She wouldn't be reminded at every turn of what she had lost. Every flower, every blade of grass—Jean-Luc, the gardener, her lover, had tended them all.

She didn't want to dwell on those weeks and months that had followed. Even now, six years later, she could still remember the twisting pain that had accompanied her every waking moment. And there had been dreams— such dreams! Taunting her with their familiarity so that it had felt as if he were still with her, still loving her...

Rachel smoothed the finely knitted dress over her hips. She glanced in the hall mirror and wondered if she had overdone the lipstick. Was it too red? Too bright? Too much an indication that she was trying to impress? Rachel opened her clutch bag and pulled out a tissue, wiping the colour from her lips. That was better. She looked paler now, more fragile, more like her usual self.

Rachel pulled open the door with trembling fingers. Jean-Luc had come himself to fetch her, and had not merely sent his chauffeur, as she'd expected. He stood some distance away with his back to her, surveying the sweeping gravelled front which had looked so pristine in his time here as a gardener but which was now weedy and in need of a massive amount of care and attention.

'The place looks rather sorry for itself now, doesn't it?' He turned and cast dark eyes over Rachel's figure. It took all of his considerable self-possession not to reveal his pleasure at the sight of her. She looked stunning, as different from his earlier meeting with her as night was from day. Here was a glimpse of the sophisticated, astute career woman he had heard about.

'You're ready?' His smile was brief, almost curt, a dark brow raised questioningly. 'We should get going. A table has been booked for eight-thirty.'

'Where are we going?' Rachel's voice was faint in comparison to his. She cleared her throat and added in stronger tones, 'Is it far?'

'Twenty kilometres or so, I believe.' Jean-Luc's response was polite but cool. 'This area does not have a particularly good choice of restaurants.'

She followed him to his car—a different one from this afternoon, she realised, larger and even more impressive, if that were possible. The chauffeur removed himself from behind the steering-wheel and opened the rear door for Rachel with a brief smile.

Jean-Luc got in beside her. Rachel shifted her position so that she sat as far away as possible from him, and made a pretence of looking out of the window.

'The windows need repainting, do they not?' Rachel glanced across at Jean-Luc, sensing the mockery in his tone. 'You must be sorry to see the place so run-down,' he added.

'It still has charm,' Rachel replied stiffly. 'It's still my home.'

'But for how much longer?' He leant forward, indicating to the chauffeur that they should be on their way.

'Isn't all this...' Rachel glanced around the plush

interior, her gaze taking in the driver ahead '…a little…extreme?'

'In what respect?' Jean-Luc's gaze was steady upon Rachel's face.

'It doesn't matter.' She shook her blonde head and glanced out of the window again. 'I just never imagined I'd see you riding around in a chauffeur-driven limousine, that's all,' she murmured.

'You never imagined that you would see me again,' Jean-Luc replied. 'I can understand why this has come as something of a shock to you.'

'Oh, you can, can you?' Rachel surveyed his handsome face with narrowed blue eyes. 'How clever you are!'

'Rachel—'

'Don't! I'm not interested!' She swallowed, struggling against a throat that was tight with unshed tears. 'I'm only here because of the Grange. Nothing else! That's all I'm interested in. Not how you became a success, or what you've been doing in the intervening years. Only the Grange.' She hardened her expression, turning briefly to look into the face she had once loved so much. 'Do you understand?'

He didn't reply immediately, simply looked deep into her eyes, making her suffer with the intensity of his gaze—so provocative, so full of power and authority. 'Oh, I understand,' he murmured. 'More than you would imagine.'

There was little Rachel wanted to say on their way to the restaurant. The silence wasn't particularly comfortable or companionable, but Rachel was damned if she'd struggle to fill the emptiness which sat so uneasily between them.

As she might have expected, the restaurant—situated in the main street of a picturesque country town, small and elegantly decorated—was of a high standard. The

car drew up outside and they were greeted in the manner
to which Jean-Luc had so clearly become accustomed.

'We'd like to order immediately.' Jean-Luc told the
waiter as he showed them to their table. He turned to
Rachel. 'You still like scallops, I take it?' She nodded.
'Wild mushrooms?'

'Yes.'

He ordered for both of them in ten seconds flat, casting a cursory glance at the menu, choosing wine with
the ease of someone who had done it a thousand times
before.

'I am capable of ordering for myself!'

'You do not like the food I have chosen?' He raised
his arm to summon the waiter.

'No, it's fine!' Rachel wished she had kept her mouth
shut. She took a sip of mineral water and glanced around
at her surroundings, anywhere except at Jean-Luc's
handsome face.

'You have been here before?'

'No.'

'It has a good atmosphere, don't you think? But the
decor is a little…'

'Insipid?' Rachel murmured, automatically noting
what she would do to improve things.

'Yes.' Jean-Luc nodded in agreement. 'Exactly that.
But we didn't come here to discuss this restaurant's
decoration, did we? You will have given a great deal of
thought to the future of the Grange over the past couple
of weeks.'

'Yes, of course.'

'You will lose it, you realise that?'

'It seems a distinct possibility.' Rachel worked hard
at sounding as businesslike and as cool as possible. If
Jean-Luc could do it, why couldn't she? She continued
to speak swiftly, refusing her brain time to conjure up a
whole host of very good reasons. 'Although I haven't

entirely given up hope that the bank will give me some more time,' she continued.

'You should.' Dark eyes gazed penetratingly at her. 'Give up hope,' he added bluntly, when Rachel raised a brow in query. 'The Grange is a lost cause—'

'If that's so, why are you here now, talking to me?' Rachel cut in swiftly. 'Why are you bothering?'

'If you will allow me to finish...' Jean-Luc paused, and took a sip of mineral water, increasing Rachel's nervous anticipation with the length of his delay. Whether he did so for effect, to produce the biggest re-action, or simply because he was working out a way to frame his next sentence, Rachel wasn't sure. 'I believe,' he asserted, 'that the Grange would make an ideal high-class hotel, health resort and conference centre.'

She knew, even as half her brain railed against the idea, that Jean-Luc's idea was viable. Her hotel and busi-ness acumen couldn't be disregarded just because the Grange happened to be her home. She tried, though, she tried very hard to dispute it. 'You are joking, surely?' she replied.

'Not at all.' Ebony eyes held hers. 'I never joke about business.'

'You really think that's the miracle plan that's going to save the day?' Rachel shook her blonde head, staring stubbornly down at the table so that Jean-Luc shouldn't read her thoughts. Her mind was already assessing the possibilities, swiftly redesigning the interior to accom-modate guest bedrooms and restaurants and leaping ahead to conference suites and leisure facilities.

'I don't remember mentioning miracles,' Jean-Luc re-sponded crisply, 'just a business proposition that would be beneficial to both of us.'

'You honestly think I could consider such a pro-posal?' Rachel's voice was tinged with half-hearted dis-belief. 'That I would want to enter into some sort of partnership with you?'

'You know, Rachel...' Jean-Luc lifted his glass and took a mouthful of wine '...that my proposition is the only thing capable of getting you out of this mess. I know you do—I can see it in your eyes.'

'Can you, indeed?' Rachel said through gritted teeth. 'How clever of you!'

He raised a dark brow, his gaze steady and unflinching. 'You're not interested?'

'There's got to be another way!' Rachel asserted. 'How can you sit there and tell me that the best thing would be to turn the Grange into a huge hotel? It's my home!'

'Not for very much longer!' Jean-Luc's voice was clipped. 'You know as well as I do that the Grange, in its present condition with all of its natural assets, is an ideal site—'

'It isn't a "site", as you so callously call it,' Rachel cut in. She gulped a breath. 'I've lived there ever since my parents were killed—'

'And now dear Aunt Clara is dead and the Grange is your responsibility! You were orphaned at a young age—that is tragic. Car accidents are tragic, death is tragic.' He lifted his broad shoulders in, it seemed to Rachel, an uncaring shrug. 'So is bankruptcy.'

Rachel pushed her plate aside. The mushrooms were good, but suddenly she had no stomach for them. She loved her work. The excitement and challenge of managing a hotel from day to day, when just about anything could happen and often did, gave her more satisfaction than she could say, but this shocking idea, that somehow she and Jean-Luc should have a shared interest—and in the Grange of all places—was difficult to contemplate. She shook her head again. 'I cannot imagine a worse scenario!'

'Except, perhaps, the one where you sack Naomi and the rest of the staff, pack up, move out and hand over the keys of the Grange to the bank?' Jean-Luc picked up his wine glass. 'You find *that* particular course of action more acceptable, do you?' There was a tense silence. 'Are you so naïve?' Jean-Luc continued remorselessly. 'What do you imagine the bank will do once they take possession?'

Rachel glanced down at her lap, avoiding his penetrating gaze. 'I haven't thought that far ahead.'

'Well, it's time you did! They'll sell to the highest bidder. They won't be concerned whether it's split up into apartments or turned into the biggest conference centre in Europe!'

'I haven't lost it yet!' Rachel persisted stubbornly. 'There's still time.'

'There's no time. Your aunt used up all the time and left you with nothing but debts,' Jean-Luc informed her brutally. 'You will be left with nothing.'

'So, why do you care?'

Why, indeed? But he did—more than he cared to admit.

He looked at her, cold and hard and formidable. 'I don't. I have been looking for suitable properties in this area for some time. In fact, I was about to close a deal when I heard of your aunt's death and subsequent problems.'

'Oh! So...so your predatory instincts took over! How extremely fortuitous that the Grange got into difficulties when it did!' Rachel replied unsteadily. 'I'm sure your shareholders are going to be very impressed at such easy pickings!'

'I have no shareholders,' Jean-Luc informed her with a cold expression. 'I own the company lock, stock and barrel.'

'Oh, well, even better!' Rachel continued scathingly. 'Think of all those profits just for yourself—you'll be a millionaire in no time!'

'I already am one!' The terse statement came as he pushed back his chair and rose from the table, throwing his napkin onto the plate in front of him in disgust. 'I'm not prepared to put up with this. It's clear from your behaviour that you're not capable of taking my proposition seriously. That is your mistake and you will have to live with the consequences.'

Rachel stared up at him in horror. 'You're leaving?' she asked. 'Just like that?'

'I see no reason to stay. You're clearly not interested in anything I have to say.'

Angry, tense, annoyed with himself at not being able to stay cool, he walked away, threading his broad frame through the tables of the restaurant.

Rachel sat for a moment, watching him go, stunned by his sudden departure. She didn't know what to do. She could barely think straight. Jean-Luc's words haunted her. Did she really want to lose the Grange? Did it honestly mean so little to her? She rose from the table, glancing at the other diners who, she realised belatedly, had been enjoying the cabaret, and followed Jean-Luc outside.

Rachel stood hesitatingly in the entrance to the restaurant, glad of the cooling night air on her heated skin.

What was she to do? How was she supposed to cope with this nightmare situation? He didn't care, that much was clear. He had said it, and she believed him. His only thought was to strike a deal, to make money.

Jean-Luc's first emotion was relief because there was always a risk in pushing too hard, and she might so easily have decided to go with her true instincts and reject everything, without giving a damn for the consequences.

'You'd like a lift home?'

Rachel spun around at the sound of his voice. She looked up, and felt the immediate lurch of awareness deep down in the pit of her stomach at the sight of him. 'I'd like to talk about the Grange,' she murmured.

He pushed a little harder. 'I think we've said all there is to say.'

'No.' Rachel shook her head. 'No, we haven't.' She paused. 'Maybe…maybe I was a little hasty just now…'

'Maybe?' His dark eyes pierced her.

'Is there somewhere quiet we can talk?' Rachel murmured. 'I don't particularly want to go back into the restaurant.'

'My car?'

'You have a chauffeur,' Rachel reminded him.

'Emile can go get himself something to eat.' Jean-Luc placed a guiding hand at the small of her back. 'This way. Would you like something to drink?' He pulled open a cabinet, once the chauffeur had been temporarily relieved of his duty and they were both installed in the back of the Rolls Royce. 'Vodka? Martini?'

'Just mineral water for me, please.'

Jean-Luc's smile held precious little humour. 'So that you can keep a clear head?'

'It makes sense, in the circumstances,' Rachel responded smoothly.

As far as business propositions were concerned, it was well thought-out and covered all the angles. The gist of Jean-Luc's proposal was that his company would pay off all the outstanding debts, agree to invest a substantial amount of money in the Grange and take the bulk of any profits in return.

'So, where do I fit in?' Rachel enquired eventually. It had been difficult to concentrate on much of the detail because as Jean-Luc had talked she had found her attention wandering away from the business of the house and estate towards more…immediate matters. He looked so…incredible. More mature, more compelling…more everything.

Usually so good at concentrating on business matters, Rachel's eyes had wandered as he spoke, drifting away from his mouth across the broad chest, down the length of his long, muscular legs, clad in dark trousers, then back to his face once again. It wasn't fair that he could still do this her, she thought, that it still mattered after all these years....

Rachel cursed silently, and dragged herself back to the important discussion in hand. 'I agree it all sounds perfectly feasible,' she continued in businesslike tones. 'The market's there—this area could do with a top-notch hotel and the layout of the Grange is, to a large extent, custom-made as far as the main features are concerned, but—'

'You don't seem to have paid a great deal of attention,' he replied coolly, his dark eyes meeting hers. 'I thought I'd made your involvement perfectly clear.'

'Evidently not clear enough!' Rachel retorted, annoyed by his superior tone and embarrassed by her previous inability to concentrate.

'I want you to run the hotel,' he informed her. 'That will be one of the conditions that I will insist upon.'

'What?' Rachel stared at him, her blue eyes wide with shock. 'Me?'

'I don't see anyone else in the near vicinity.' Jean-Luc's tone was dry. 'You are the obvious choice. You have been in the hotel business for the last few years, have you not?'

Rachel frowned. 'You know about that?'

'I know all the relevant details which might have some bearing on this investment.' His gaze was direct. 'You imagined that you would be able to lounge around in glamorous idleness while I wasted unnecessary money employing someone to—'

'I do not lounge around! I have never lounged around!' Rachel stormed. 'I work.'

'You are currently managing a small hotel in the Cotswolds, I believe? It will be easy enough for you to work through your notice while the Grange is being refurbished. I do not know why you are looking at me like that,' he commented smoothly. 'It seems an eminently suitable arrangement. The Grange will still be your home, after all, and as you already have suitable experience in the hotel profession this will give you something worthwhile to direct your energies to.

'You will have help of course,' he added. 'I already have in mind an employee who will suit the position of assistant manager. He is efficient, reliable, English…' a flicker of a smile '…but I try not to hold that against him.'

'You're pleased that this has happened, aren't you?' Rachel declared shakily. 'You're not really interested in turning this into a profitable business. You just want to…to humiliate me!'

'I'm saving your family home and offering you a job into the bargain—I don't see where humiliation comes into it!' he replied crisply. 'Now, I suggest you drop the pathetic accusations and stop wasting time! I will have my solicitor draw up an agreement, which you will find fair—not to mention generous. Tomorrow afternoon you can sign and then everything will be able to proceed without delay.'

'I don't actually recall hearing myself agreeing to any of this!' Rachel snapped.

'But you will.' Jean-Luc's gaze was compelling as he turned to look at her. 'Won't you?'

CHAPTER THREE

NAOMI was over the moon about the last-minute reprieve for the Grange, and couldn't see anything wrong with the proposal.

'The place will still be in the family, where it belongs,' she replied firmly, serving Rachel breakfast the following morning. 'That's the main thing. You might not have complete control but, in the circumstances, it's just about the best any of us could have hoped for. You say this man has guaranteed us jobs in the new venture?'

'Yes.' Rachel spooned a piece of grapefruit into her mouth discontentedly.'If you want them. The new regime might be a little different from the old one, however.'

'He's a bit of a looker, isn't he?' Naomi bustled around the large kitchen with an ebullient air. She grinned at Rachel, her brown eyes twinkling mischievously. 'If I were thirty years younger! Actually, I'll tell you who he reminds me of...' she continued. 'You remember that French boy—the one you had a bit of a crush on?'

'What?' Rachel pushed the half-eaten grapefruit away from her. 'Oh...yes,' she murmured.

'This man's different, of course—'

'In what way?' Rachel couldn't keep the edge from her voice.

Naomi cast her a frowning glance. 'Well...he's rich, for one thing. Sophisticated. And he's not French.'

'No?'

'Is he, then? There wasn't a hint of accent when he spoke to me the other day.' Naomi, cloth in hand, began to wipe over the kitchen surfaces with vigour. 'Very cultural tones. I wish more people spoke the Queen's English the way that young man does.' She paused, staring across the kitchen at a point above Rachel's head.

'Yes…' she murmured, 'quite the sort of man your aunt would have approved of. He'll not do anything to harm the old place.'

'You think so?' Rachel struggled to keep her irritation under control.

'Well, he won't be allowed to, will he? After all there is such a thing as planning and good taste. And you're going to be here in charge of everything.' Naomi waved her cloth in Rachel's direction. 'No, it will turn out all right, you'll see. I've got a good feeling about all of this.'

Rachel rose from the kitchen table, and carried her bowl and cup across to the dishwasher. She could hardly believe the conversation they were having. The awful irony of it! A small part of her was tempted to reveal the truth of Jean-Luc's identity, but only a small part. Just thinking about him made her feel miserably confused, angry, upset…

Naomi would find out about him eventually, she was bound to, but Rachel would be more than happy if that occasion was a long time in the future. When—if there ever was going to be a when—she herself had come to terms with Jean-Luc's involvement in her life, albeit on a purely commercial basis.

'I've got to get ready,' Rachel murmured. 'I don't want to be late.'

'Your navy suit is cleaned and pressed,' Naomi called. 'Oh, and by the way, did you see my note?'

Rachel paused at the kitchen door. 'What note?'

'I left it on the hall table. Shaun called again last evening.'

'Did he?' Rachel frowned. 'What did you tell him?'

'That you were out. He says he'll drop by,' Naomi

added. 'I must say, he sounded more than a little upset. Mind you he was pleased when I told him about the new developments.'

Naomi, never particularly sensitive to other people's moods, ignored Rachel's look of dismay and continued cheerfully. 'I said the situation was really looking far more hopeful with regard to the house and estate, and that things were moving at a pace, and that all the tension that had been affecting you lately would soon be gone and that might mean that you and he—'

'Naomi...' Rachel ran a hand through her tousled blonde locks, debating whether now was a good time to tell her that she really had to start minding her own business—even if Shaun was her great-nephew. 'You shouldn't have talked like that to Shaun. I don't want him knowing my business and, apart from anything else, nothing's settled yet, and even if it were—'

'But it will be.' Naomi resumed her cleaning with a satisfied smile. 'It will be very soon though, won't it?'

'Yes, but that's not the point...' Rachel released a tense breath. She wasn't sure if she was going to be able to cope with all the tension and anxiety the day ahead was undoubtedly going to bring. Having to spend time with Jean-Luc was going to be difficult enough, without the complication of Shaun trying to make contact again.

'I'll get dressed.' Rachel gave up. It was no use trying to make Naomi see the error of her ways now. She glanced at the kitchen clock. She didn't have the time for anything more—there were far more pressing things on the agenda.

The rest of the day disappeared in a blur of anxious trepidation. The trustees of her aunt's estate, solicitors, the bank—everyone—were more than happy with the arrangement offered by Jean-Luc and his powerful company, and, despite Rachel's innumerable reservations, they urged her to accept. In financial terms at least, it was clearly an offer that couldn't be refused.

She fled home from the offices in town once the papers were signed and sealed. It was late afternoon, and she desperately needed time on her own to come to terms with all that had happened—and all that was about to happen in the future.

She hardly dared to look too far ahead. It was impossible to predict anything. Jean-Luc's deal *was* generous—she had been made to see that by the bank manager and the trustees. Profit, despite the accusations she'd flung at him last night, seemed to be taking a back seat. So what were his motives in all of this? Why come to the rescue? What did he hope to gain?

The questions kept spinning round and round in Rachel's head until she almost felt dizzy with the speed of them. The biggest and most important question was, of course, why he had returned. *Why?*

She loved the old orchard—one of her favourite places on the estate. The buds were just beginning to show white on the gnarled apple trees. Rachel, having changed from the business suit of the day, was now dressed in a snug woollen cardigan and dark trousers in a matching shade of green. She walked slowly, breathing in the fresh spring air and thinking about what needed to be done.

She'd have to hand in her notice at the hotel almost immediately. From the talk at the meeting this morning, Jean-Luc wanted everything to proceed as swiftly as possible. The Grange was to open by the end of summer, and that meant a lot of work—both for the planners and building contractors, as well as for herself, if everything was going to be ready on time.

Rachel thought about recruitment—that was going to be high on the list of priorities. People were the mainstay of any organisation and she needed to make sure they got the best that were available. And what about the look of the place? She paused, turning to glance across at the imposing exterior of her home. Country house, yes, but not *too* country house, not *too* predictable. The Grange needed to have its own style, something people would remember long after they had left.

The daffodils were at their best, crisp and cheerful, great swathes of them as far as the eye could see. Rachel inhaled a steadying breath. She was going too fast. It had only been a day since Jean-Luc had dropped this bombshell on her, and here she was, planning and organising things already.

A lone blackbird warbled tunefully in a branch overhead. Rachel looked up and watched him sing, glad of the momentary diversion. Turning the Grange into a hotel *was* a good idea. She could admit that now she was over the initial shock. It was just Jean-Luc's involvement that was so difficult to handle. She needed to focus on her own professional expertise to prevent herself from dwelling on the personal minefield which undoubtedly lay ahead, to concentrate on what she was good at, on what she loved doing—that was the best way.

She had to be strong. OK, so as soon as she'd set eyes on him it had been as if the clock hadn't moved a second. She felt... Rachel slowly shook her head. She felt just the same attraction for him as she had ever done, purely physical attraction, of course—she didn't *like* him any more, certainly didn't love him the way she once had, she told herself firmly—but this...thrill she felt whenever she set eyes on him, that was bad enough.

Did he have an ulterior motive? Of course he did. She had grown up fast once she had realized that their affair had been little more than a holiday romance—an intense one undoubtedly, passionate, overwhelming, but one that had held no future. She had been made to understand the full extent of her naïvety with every lonely day that had passed. Gone was the time when she trusted so easily, accepted what people said at face value—Jean-Luc had made sure of that.

Jean-Luc walked resolutely through the orchard, almost oblivious of his surroundings, his gaze fixed on Rachel's figure ahead. There were a thousand things he could be doing—all of them important but not, he thought as he watched her from a distance, as important or urgent as this…

She looked so beautiful standing there. So perfect. What was she thinking about? He saw her turn and look up at the Grange. Yes, it would be this place, her home. The thing that mattered most. Jean-Luc watched her quietly, dwelling on thoughts about the past…

Would things have turned out differently if he hadn't returned home to France for those few days? It was a question that he had asked himself over and over again, and one to which he simply had no answer.

On the Friday evening he had received an urgent call from home, telling him that his father was ill. Rachel had been away for the weekend, visiting an old friend. He himself had encouraged her to go, he remembered, had been so confident, so naïve, so foolishly in love… He had rushed home to France, leaving a note for Rachel. There had been no doubt in his mind that she would be here at the Grange, waiting for him, on his return—no doubt at all. When she hadn't been…

Six years was a long time, but he could still picture her aunt's rather triumphant expression as she announced that Rachel, in his absence, had decided to take an unexpected, but much-wanted trip to America to visit distant relations, and would not be returning to the Grange for some weeks.

His reaction to this extraordinary piece of news was marked with concern and not a little suspicion. He was young and angry and in love—it didn't take a genius to work out that her aunt had played a powerful part in instigating what felt like their enforced separation, and there was an angry exchange between himself and the old woman.

His dismissal didn't bother him—it was something that would have happened sooner rather than later, given the old woman's growing dislike of him. What did bother him was the silence from Rachel. He spent hours searching high and low, without finding any evidence of a letter or note. Not a word of explanation as to why she should go away.

How long was it before he accepted her absence as the rejection it was? Days, weeks, months, maybe never?

She wrote to him eventually once he was back home in France, a letter, postmarked England, which caused him so much pain and anguish that to reflect upon it even now... Jean-Luc's jaw tightened. It had been full of thanks and passionate gratitude, but also heartless in its dismissal of a future he had thought they were both destined to share.

He had considered going back—talking to her face to face—but his pain had still been too raw, his anger at being rejected too intense to contemplate such a move. He had buried everything deep down, closing the lid firmly on the experience—pretending almost that it had never happened, forcing himself to get on with his life so that he could forget her. Except, of course, it hadn't been that easy.

He inhaled deeply and continued walking.

'Naomi said I'd find you here.'

Rachel swung around at the sound of Jean-Luc's voice. Like her, he had changed out of the dark business suit of the day, and was now dressed in less formal attire. She tried not to notice how much more he looked like the old Jean-Luc as he walked towards her, clad in denims and a chunky beige sweater that accentuated his tanned skin and dark features.

'What do you want?' She had hoped she might be more able to control her antagonistic tendencies now that the first shock of seeing Jean-Luc again had faded, but they resurfaced as soon as she heard the sound of his voice and found herself being caught by the formidable intensity of his brown eyes.

'Now, is that any way to talk to your partner?'

'Am I supposed to find that remark amusing?' Rachel replied coolly. 'We're not partners—not in any sense.'

'Clearly you weren't paying as much attention as I supposed this morning.' His expression revealed cool humour. He turned to look at the Grange, mellow in the soft afternoon light. 'This is a joint venture.'

'On paper, maybe!'

'On paper, in reality.' Jean-Luc raised dark brows. 'In every way there is. Oh, incidentally, Naomi's worried about your intake of food. She asked me to tell you that there's a cold platter waiting for you if you feel in need of sustenance.'

'I don't!' Rachel's voice was taut and hard. 'I haven't got much of an appetite at the moment!'

'It's the turmoil and upheaval of the past few weeks…' Jean-Luc's voice was smooth and assured. 'You'll begin to feel better now that everything's settled.'

'*Settled?*' Rachel looked at his handsome face in astonishment. 'Are you serious?'

His eyes held hers for a long moment. 'Completely.'

Rachel gave a derisive shake of her head and turned away because to look into those hypnotic eyes was torture of the worst kind. 'I can't believe you're doing this to me.'

'You make it sound like some kind of assault.'

'Why have you come here?' Rachel spun round to face him. There was a hint of desperation in her expression. '*Why?*'

'We've covered this ground before.'

'Have we? Oh, yes! You were just passing and you happened to notice I was in need of a couple of million pounds and so you thought—hey, why not help an old friend?' Rachel's voice sounded harsh. She closed her eyes for a moment and inhaled slowly. She didn't want to feel this way, all knotted and twisted and tormented inside.

'We were never old friends.'

'No.' Her voice was low, a little ragged.

'My motives—what you imagine them to be—are irrelevant.' Jean-Luc's tone was chillingly smooth. 'We have entered into a contract, one that is fair and which you have no need to be worried about—'

'*Worried?*' Rachel's voice was quiet. She paced the orchard. 'Why should I be worried?' she asked wearily. 'My home is about to be rearranged around my ears. I'm being forced into leaving a job that I love! What on earth have I got to worry about?'

'Very little now that I've come to your rescue!' Jean-Luc replied sharply. 'I don't expect or want gratitude, but an attempt at making the best of the situation would seem like the sensible thing to do.' He considered her flushed face for a moment. 'Can you stand there before me and swear that there is not a part of you that's excited at the prospect of this challenge?'

Rachel hesitated for a moment, before replying as honestly as she could. 'OK, then, yes, you're right. I have been giving the practicalities some thought, and it is going to be a challenge, but that doesn't mean I'm happy at your involvement—not in any way, shape or form,' she added, just so that he would be left in no doubt. 'There were other people to consider—people who supported Aunt Clara over many years. I had no choice.'

She spoke coolly, forcing herself to sound as business-like as possible, holding herself upright as she looked straight into his far too handsome face. Acting—acting all the time.

'I agree your options were limited,' Jean-Luc agreed, 'but I am confident that our partnership will work effectively. Deep down, you must know that you have done the right thing.'

'By allowing you back into my life?' Rachel's response was automatic, a thought spoken aloud.

'Is this how it's going to be every time I come here?' Jean-Luc queried. 'I had hoped to keep our personal—'

'You...you won't be visiting often?' The agonising prospect stilled Rachel's mobile features. Her voice was strained. 'Surely there's no need for that?'

'There's every need.' His voice was firm. 'I am investing a considerable sum of money into this project. I can see now that there is going to be a need for careful monitoring.'

'But surely you don't need to... I mean, you have staff to do that sort of thing.'

'Yes, of course. But, you see...' Jean-Luc's mouth twisted chillingly. 'I suddenly find myself with a need for a change, a new challenge. It's been a long while since I've been involved in a project at grass-roots level. Clinching deals, holding board meetings, discussing finance—all of them give a certain amount of satisfaction, but now...' he looked at her consideringly '...I find that it is not enough. Stunned, Rachel—or simply overwhelmed with excitement at the prospect?'

'But you told me...' She cleared her throat and tried again, hardening her voice as best she could. 'You led me to believe that there would be little personal involvement.'

'I've changed my mind.' Jean-Luc's mouth curved into an assured smile. He glanced around the orchard. 'Years dull the memory—I had forgotten how beautiful this place can be.'

'Why are you doing this to me?' Rachel whispered. 'Why are you being so—?'

'Determined?' Dark brows were raised in query. A bitter smile marred the attractive line of his mouth. 'Gone is the weak-willed youth who cut the grass and tended the flower borders. When I left this microcosm of Olde England all those years ago I promised myself several things—most of those promises have helped me become the man you see before you now.'

'An unprincipled and arrogant swine, you mean?' Rachel said unsteadily. She was trembling with anger but, of course, there was more to it than that. Jean-Luc looked lethal, standing before her. The strength of him, the unleashed virility and passion which was so much an integral part of him, was like a tangible force that kept her rooted to the spot.

'Most possibly.' His voice was low, controlled, but not without a startling intensity sent shivers down Rachel's spine. 'I don't want to fight,' he added. 'You have to believe that if we are to make this thing work.'

It took Rachel several moments before she could reply. 'I…I want to believe it…' She looked into his handsome face, her eyes glistening with unshed tears. 'But you must understand that this…is difficult for me. After all these years…' Rachel shook her head. She steeled herself to be brave. 'I never expected to see you again,' she whispered.

'Nor I you.'

There was a long moment of silence. Jean-Luc seemed to be debating whether to say something. Was he going to apologise for the way he had treated her all those years ago? Rachel wondered. Did she want that? Would it make her feel any better?

But when he eventually spoke there was precious little sign of remorse or apology. 'You're going to need to move out while the Grange is being refurbished,' he announced. 'Have you thought about that? Where you might stay?'

Rachel shook her head. She should have known. He wasn't the sort of man to apologise. 'No,' she breathed, trying hard to focus on the here and now instead of what had once been. 'No, I haven't.' She turned from him, releasing a sigh of tension.

'There's the old lodge,' she murmured, glancing through the trees. 'It's not in a bad state of repair...' Now that the idea had entered her head, it seemed a good one. 'Yes,' she added in stronger tones, 'that would be suitable. It's always been well maintained I used to ask Aunt Clara why she didn't bother to rent it out.'

'She clearly wasn't keen on making money.' Jean-Luc's voice was dry. 'Only spending it.'

Rachel chose to ignore this comment, true as it was. 'I'll stay in the lodge,' she confirmed. 'It will be perfect.'

'Are you sure? You said it was in a good state of repair, but when was the last time you visited it?'

'Oh...' Rachel lifted her shoulders in a slight shrug. 'A couple of years ago, I suppose.' She remembered the occasion well. She had been dwelling in the past, as she was wont to do when she felt miserable, thinking of Jean-Luc. Remembering. The lodge had been one of their places—or at least that was how she had thought of it. She had avoided it like the plague for the previous few years. Not that it had made much difference—she had still spent far too long thinking about him.

'A couple of years?' Jean-Luc looked sceptical. 'I think that maybe we ought to pay it a visit.'

Rachel didn't bother to hide her surprise. 'Now?'

'Why not?'

She could think of a hundred reasons. 'You've surely got better things to do with your time.'

'Not for the rest of the day I haven't. Is the key still kept in the usual place?'

He remembered. And he didn't mind Rachel knowing

that he did. She tried to banish the memory of candle-lit evenings, spent lying together in each other's arms on rugs and cushions purloined from the big house. 'Yes...' She tried hard not let him see how difficult this was for her. 'As far as I know.'

'Let's go, then.'

It was a mistake, of course. She should have just said no to Jean-Luc. He didn't care. Not at all. This latest torture was, for all she knew, another clever, rather more subtle way of making her suffer.

The key was discovered beneath a pile of old leaves and rubbish. Jean-Luc inserted it into the lock and stood aside to allow Rachel entry.

It was a pleasant sunny spring afternoon, and the tiny house had a cheerful air, despite the fact that it hadn't been inhabited for many years. Rachel walked to a window and opened it wide, and immediately a gust of crisp, fresh air breezed into the room. She leant her elbows on the stone window-sill and looked across at the shock of yellow daffodils blowing in the orchard.

These first few moments were more difficult than even she had anticipated. Behind her, Jean-Luc's footsteps could be heard slowly pacing the room.

'It's smaller than I remember.' His voice was deep, rough-edged.

Rachel kept her gaze fixed on the orchard. Her whole body was rigid with tension. Her chest felt tight, she could hardly breathe. *Don't think! Don't think!* she told herself.

'Like a doll's house, compared with the Grange, but not without charm. I remember...' He paused. 'Didn't you at one time consider living here?'

'I thought about it.' Her voice was tight. 'But Aunt Clara said how ridiculous it would be for me to live here when there were so many rooms at the Grange. She seemed quite upset that I should even consider the idea so I forgot all about it. I didn't want to upset her.'

'No, of course not.'

Rachel breathed a lungful of fresh air, and then turned to face Jean-Luc. 'Meaning?' she enquired with an arched brow.

'Only what I said—that you never wanted to upset your aunt.' His gaze was unflinching. 'She was an important part of your life.'

'Yes.' Rachel refused to crumble under his gaze. 'She was.'

Jean-Luc glanced up at the ceiling. 'I think we should go upstairs and see what sort of state the roof is in. I can bring in builders straight away, if necessary.'

'You go.' Rachel spun back around and looked out of the window again. 'I'll stay here.'

'I don't think so.' Jean-Luc came up from behind and, placing both hands on Rachel's waist, spoke in one ear. His voice dropped to a husky drawl, challenging, assertive, dangerous… 'You are the one who is possibly going to live here over the next few months so I think the least you could do is show a little interest.'

She couldn't move, even if she had wanted to, not while he was so close. She could smell the fresh scent of his cologne and feel the strength of his body, lean and muscular, through the softness of her clothes. It was all too familiar, all too much. 'OK.' Rachel forced her voice to sound cool and vaguely disinterested. 'I can manage that.' She waited, holding her breath until the moment when Jean-Luc put distance between their two bodies. His smile, when she finally looked into his face, told her more than she wanted to know. He knew. He understood how easy it was to unnerve and upset her. The intensity of his dark brown eyes, the proximity of his body, told her he knew.

'Ceiling looks fine!' Rachel, making a great effort, spoke in no-nonsense tones as she regarded the larger of the two upstairs rooms a moment later.

'This is the best bedroom. And it's got a good view

over the orchard and rear drive. It just needs cleaning and decorating and then I'll be able to bring some furniture over from the house—not the best stuff,' she added, throwing a glance at Jean-Luc who was staring out of another window, and seemed particularly disinterested in what she was saying. 'I imagine you'll want that for the hotel.'

Silence. Rachel waited. 'Did you hear what I said?'

He turned then, looking at her with a watchful air. 'Naomi asked me to give you a message earlier.'

'Oh?'

'You had a phone call.'

Rachel feigned disinterest. 'Did I?'

'Aren't you going to ask who from—that's the usual response?' Jean-Luc enquired. His voice was cool, with a hint of steel in his gaze. 'It was from someone called Shaun. He's very keen to get in touch with you, apparently.'

'Is he?'

'You're seeing him.'

Rachel stopped pacing, and stared at Jean-Luc. 'What makes you think that?'

'Naomi mentioned it.'

'Did she?' Rachel shook her head. 'Well, she had no right!' Her natural instinct was to tell Jean-Luc the truth about herself and Shaun but, then, she told herself, why on earth should she? It was finished and it was final, but there was no reason why Jean-Luc should know that. 'Thank you for passing the message on,' she continued shakily.

'Oh, it was the least I could do. Apparently, you and he are made for each other.' The mockery in his tone was obvious. 'What's the matter?' His handsome features had taken on a hard, cynical expression. 'You don't look particularly pleased. Have I spoken out of turn? Naomi led me to believe that you two were very close.'

'As I said, she had no right!'

'She doesn't remember me.' Jean-Luc's voice held a thread of amusement.

'No, she doesn't.'

'Why haven't you told her?'

'Because...' Rachel shook her head and turned away. As her eyes misted with tears the daffodils glistened and merged in the distance. 'I couldn't see the point.'

'I'm much admired.' Jean-Luc strolled across the room toward Rachel. 'Or, at least, my wealth is. Naomi can't do enough to please—ironic, don't you think?'

'Not particularly, no.'

'You don't find her attitude a little sickening—or should I say sycophantic?' he challenged.

'My! How your English has improved!' Rachel didn't know how to defend Naomi against such an unmistakable fact—she herself had found the old woman's attitude more than a little hard to take, especially when she allowed herself to remember all the snide comments and difficulties she had thrown at them both six years ago.

'I always spoke good English. Surely you remember that? It isn't such a long time ago since we—'

'I did not come here to reminisce about old times!' Rachel's voice shook. 'In fact,' she added, with more than a hint of desperation, 'I was a fool to come here at all!'

'Rachel!' She didn't reply when he called her. She was fleeing, her feet clattering on the wooden treads of the stairs. He called again and she ran all the faster, conscious of the sound of Jean-Luc's footsteps behind her.

She caught her hand on the edge of the door as she swung through it out into the open air and gave a cry of pain, but didn't bother to stop and examine it. Instead, she continued to run along the overgrown path and out into the orchard, her legs scything through the field of daffodils, her blonde hair streaming out behind.

'*Rachel!*' She tripped and almost fell, her arms and

legs flailing. She found her footing, but by then the
ground between them had been eaten up by the speed
and length of Jean-Luc's stride. He caught her and held
her arms, turning her towards him with a slow and determined air. 'What is it? Why do you run?'

'I run because I don't want to spend any more time
in that house with you!' She glared up into his handsome
face. 'Let go of me!' she cried.

'You're upset.'

'Of course I'm upset!' Rachel, breathing hard, struggled to restrain her emotions. 'What did you expect?'
She glanced down at her stinging hand as he released
her and saw, to her surprise, a great deal of blood, seep-
ing from her wound. Jean-Luc saw it, too.

'Mon Dieu!'

'It's all right!' Rachel tried to turn away, but he
caught her arm.

'No, it is not.' His accent in that moment was more
pronounced, as it had been in the old days. Hearing it
was almost more than Rachel could bear. Jean-Luc
reached into his trouser pocket and produced a clean
handkerchief, pressing it gently over her hand. 'How did
you do this?'

'I caught it on the door.' She shook her head, conscious of tears which were welling up inside. 'A nail or
something—it will be all right.' She kept her gaze firmly
fixed on her hand.

'You are upset.' For the first time since he had returned his voice held a huskiness that revealed real sympathy. 'Don't cry,' he murmured. 'If I said something to
make this happen then I am sorry.' He tilted her chin
with one finger so that he could look into her glistening
eyes. 'Truly.'

'It doesn't matter.' Rachel wondered why she both-
ered to lie. Everything about her face, her body language, revealed that the opposite was true. Everything
mattered where Jean-Luc was concerned. A sob rose un-

expectedly from her throat and completed the obvious-
ness of the lie.

There was a moment in which he did nothing, fighting
against himself—against instincts which seemed only
destined to bring him to his knees. Madness! he thought
as he held her close, wrapping her in the circle of his
arms. Utter madness.

Rachel closed her eyes and did her utmost to combat
the tears, but it was so difficult with Jean-Luc's arms
around her. How long had she yearned for this? A thousand—ten thousand times since that dreadful day when
she had arrived home and discovered him gone? Another
sob followed the first. She gulped, working hard at holding back the torrent of tears that threatened to over-
whelm her.

He released her after a long moment. Rachel raised
her head from his chest, unsure of her ability to continue
with the façade of not wanting him. One look at her
expression and surely he would see, understand, the
depth of her desire?

'You need to clean the wound.' His voice was matter-
of-fact, not cold exactly but lacking the warmth of a
moment ago. He hardly looked at her. 'You should go
to the house and bathe it in disinfectant.' Jean-Luc
stepped away, glancing with unseeing eyes at his wrist-
watch as he did so. 'I have things to do—an appointment.' He glanced at her briefly. 'Will you be all right?'

'Yes.' Rachel nodded. 'Jean-Luc?'

But it was too late. Rachel frowned, watching as he
turned away and strode through the daffodils towards the
Grange.

CHAPTER FOUR

'SHAUN, I don't know what you think you're doing here. But I've already told you that there's little point!'

'I've come to apologise.'

'For what? You haven't done anything.' Rachel, wrapped up against the chill wind in a long, dark, ankle-length coat, tried to contain her annoyance. 'Shaun, please! Just leave me alone.'

'Rachel, you don't understand!' Shaun stopped walking and turned toward her, blocking her path so that she had to stand still and listen to him. 'I know our relationship hit a sticky patch, but if you'll give it another chance.' Shaun's pale face was earnest. 'You must know that I very much want us to try again. I understand why you said the things you did, but—'

'If you understand then you must be able to see that nothing has changed.' Rachel inhaled a steadying breath, conscious that she had said these words before. She shook her blonde head, clad as it was now in a woollen hat. 'I like you, Shaun, but—'

'You like me! So, what's the problem? Hell, Rachel, you must know I don't prostrate myself like this for every girl I meet.'

'Shaun, you really have got to stop phoning me, writing to me, visiting me!' Rachel shook her head, and saw with dismay the familiar, dark, gleaming car pull up alongside Shaun's rather more mundane vehicle. 'I'm not going to change my mind about us.'

Shaun followed her gaze. Emile, the chauffeur, appeared and opened the rear door. Jean-Luc emerged. 'This is the saviour of the Grange, I presume?' he commented sarcastically. 'Naomi talks of him as if he were a god or something.'

'He's certainly not that—just a businessman,' Rachel replied, hoping fervently that Jean-Luc would go in search of the young, extremely feminine architect who had already been here for most of the morning, rather than choose to cross the drive and speak to her. No such luck. Her heart turned over as he looked across and began to head in her direction.

'Rachel.' Jean-Luc's smile was brief and without so much as a fragment of warmth. Dressed impeccably in a fashionably cut business suit, he turned and surveyed Shaun with an enigmatic gaze. 'Aren't you going to introduce us?'

She didn't want to but, then, Rachel suspected, Jean-Luc knew as much. 'This is Shaun…Shaun Gallagher, Naomi's great-nephew. Shaun, this is Jean-Luc Manoire.'

The two men shook hands. Jean-Luc, Rachel could tell, was distinctly unimpressed by Shaun—although what exactly he had taken a dislike to she couldn't tell. He looked as smart as he ever did—a must in his job as company rep—handsome in a quieter, more restrained kind of way, with his light brown hair and more slender physique. Friendly, respectable, trustworthy…

Rachel released a sigh. Which was, of course, why she had become involved with him in the first place—a reaction to the striking, dangerous, devil-may-care lover of her youth.

'I'd like your opinion on what the architect has to say.' Jean-Luc's eyes held her face. 'You can spare the time, I presume?'

'Er…yes.' Rachel nodded, careful not to show a measure of relief. 'Shaun was just going.'

Shaun didn't like it—she sensed that immediately— not any of it. Not the way Jean-Luc dismissed him with a look, or the fact that Rachel seemed so keen to have him leave. But she couldn't help that. He had to under-stand that their relationship was well and truly over—surely he understood that by now?

Shaun looked down into Rachel's face. 'Yes, I have a client to see.'

'Well, don't let us keep you.' Jean-Luc's voice was cool and superior.

'I'll be in touch.' There was a hardness in Shaun's voice, a look in his hazel eyes which Rachel had never seen before. He took her hands in his, then bent and kissed her mouth—an unexpectedly audacious move, given the content of their conversation and the non-existent state of their relationship. 'I meant what I said,' he murmured. 'I'll speak to you soon.' Rachel, conscious of Jean-Luc's eyes boring into her, hid her annoyance as best she could, watching Shaun's departure with a composure she didn't feel.

'I expected something more—something better.'

Rachel turned to look at Jean-Luc. 'I beg your par-don?'

'I don't like him,' he continued. 'He's not right for you.'

She knew that, but it didn't help her anger at all to hear it from Jean-Luc's arrogant lips. 'I'll be the judge of that!' she replied coolly. 'And, besides, I don't recall asking you for your opinion.'

'No, but I feel inclined to give it all the same. How long have you known him?'

'Long enough!'

Jean-Luc raised dark brows. 'For what?'

Rachel watched as Shaun got into his company car and raced away down the drive. 'I told you, I won't thank you for interfering in my personal life!'

'As far as I can remember, you haven't thanked me for involving myself in any part of your life,' Jean-Luc replied dryly.

'You said something about talking to the architect?'

Rachel turned from him, wrapping her coat closely around her body as a sharp wind blew from the east. 'Am I to have my say in the way the Grange is going to be renovated, then?'

'Your opinion is of value.' Jean-Luc looked cold and unapproachable suddenly. 'Let's go inside,' he added. 'I'm already far later than I anticipated.'

'Perhaps you should relinquish the day-to-day running of the operation to someone in your employ,' Rachel replied swiftly. 'You are clearly a very busy, important man.'

He chose to ignore her retort. 'You've handed in your notice?'

'Yes, everyone was very sorry to hear that I was leaving.'

'Were they, indeed?'

Rachel caught the glimpse of a smile, and knew he was faintly amused at her expense. 'I have to work it through, of course,' she added frostily, 'so my time spent here is almost as precious as yours. I can only spare a couple of hours, then I'll have to get back.'

Rachel wondered, as they walked side by side towards the Grange, why she persisted with this futile war of words. It was getting her nowhere. Jean-Luc had decided on a course of action, and instinct told her that nothing she, or anyone else, might say would deflect him from it.

The architect, a young Frenchwoman in her late twenties, was very enthusiastic about the project. Rachel listened carefully and discovered that her fears about horrendous alterations were going to be, as Jean-Luc had repeatedly told her, unfounded.

The meeting was worthwhile, and helped to allay a lot of Rachel's worries about the Grange. The work, although extensive in parts, would be completed in stages—the main part of the house first to enable a swift and efficient opening, with the east and west wings completed later. An indoor swimming pool seemed to be high on the list of priorities, along with many additional bathrooms and general refurbishment of the interior.

She shook hands with the smart-looking woman at the end of her visit, and watched as Jean-Luc did the same. The architect had clearly met him before, and the two spoke for some little while, discussing a variety of matters unrelated to business or the Grange. It was clear she found him attractive—what woman wouldn't? Rachel reminded herself. Jean-Luc's good looks alone were enough to have women falling over themselves, but add to that his wealth, power and charm...

Rachel focused on the mobile face of the architect. She was smiling at Jean-Luc, her eyes bright and alluring, and he was returning her smile, slipping into French as he spoke so that Rachel struggled to understand more than one word in a dozen. She wondered what they were saying...

He was being more charming than was necessary, flirting just because Rachel was here. He had hated seeing that moron kissing her. It had taken a significant amount of restraint just to keep from throttling Shaun where he stood. His mind wanted to torture him, of course, but he wouldn't allow it. To have witnessed a kiss between them was bad enough. The prospect of anything else...

So here he was, acting like an idiot, feeling the pain of rejection more than ever, convincing himself—as he chatted and laughed with Yvette Chantrelle—that there were plenty of other women who found him attractive and desirable, even if Rachel didn't.

'I'll speak to you soon.' Jean-Luc, winding up the conversation with the architect, caught hold of Rachel's arm before she could walk away. 'Rachel...'

'Yes, what is it?'

He hesitated, but only for a moment. 'I'll be returning to France this evening. Here's my mobile number.' He handed Rachel a piece of paper. 'You can contact me if there's anything you want to discuss.'

'I doubt that there will be.' Rachel's voice was clipped. 'Anything to discuss with you, I mean,' she added crisply. 'You seem to have everything under control.'

'You're going to get the decorators into the lodge as soon as possible?' he queried, ignoring her pointed remark. 'It would be best if you moved out before the chaos really takes hold.'

'Chaos?' Rachel frowned.

'A bad choice of word. Not chaos,' he amended. 'But, of course, there will be a great deal of upheaval—in the short term at least.' He paused. 'I'll contact you as soon as the staff leave for the summer,' he continued. 'I'm not happy about you being left here alone.'

'I'll be fine.' Rachel refused to be affected by such unexpected compassion. 'There's no need to worry.'

Jean-Luc silently rebuked himself. 'Security is a precaution I'd prefer not to leave to chance,' he informed her in more businesslike tones. 'There are a number of valuable objects in the Grange.'

'Objects?' Rachel's voice was flat. 'Yes, of course,' she murmured wearily.

'I will speak to you in a few days.' Dark eyes seduced her, mesmerising her. 'Phone me if you need anything,' he added briskly. Then he was getting into his car and it was pulling away, and Rachel was left, standing alone, on the gravelled drive.

The lodge was looking so much better. It was surprising what a couple of skilled decorators and some paint could achieve in a couple of weeks.

Rachel finished polishing the latticed kitchen window, and looked round at all that had been achieved. Even Naomi would be pleased with the state of cleanliness— the work surfaces shone, and the old quarry tiles had a rich glow. Now that neutral carpeting had been laid in the small downstairs sitting room and the bedroom, the whole place was finished.

Rachel set off on her bike and headed back towards the Grange. She was keen to select a last couple of items—an umbrella stand, and a small oak chest for her sitting room—before the storage contractors moved in tomorrow.

The house was eerily quiet. Rachel parked her bike around the side of the building next to the kitchen door, and slipped a key into the lock.

Naomi had departed earlier that morning, keen to get away and visit her sister in Scotland. 'You know what your aunt was like,' she had said quietly, clearly somewhat reluctant to speak ill of the dead. 'She always was a bit demanding, and I never felt I could leave her for too long. So it will be a real treat—as long as you'll be fine of course. I wouldn't want to go, knowing you'll be unhappy at being left alone.'

At which point Rachel had swiftly convinced Naomi that she would not be the slightest bit unhappy, just in case she changed her mind.

Rachel had been looking forward to having time on her own. Putting on a brave and cheerful face about everything while Naomi and the rest of the staff were around had become a definite strain.

'That's all right, then. I've asked Shaun to keep an eye on you while I'm away.'

'Naomi!' Rachel's dismayed reply had been swift.

'Oh, now, don't go getting cross with me. I thought it for the best. Put my mind at rest, if no one else's. And a bit of peace and quiet might just be the very thing that the two of you need. You'll be able to sort a few things out.'

'Hardly peace and quiet,' Rachel had replied, frowning in frustration at Naomi's interference. 'The contractors are arriving first thing tomorrow.'

'Oh, well...' Naomi had looked at Rachel and shaken her. 'It's done now.'

There was someone in the kitchen. Rachel's heart sank. 'What are you doing here?'

Shaun, sitting in the easy chair by the range, grinned inanely up at her. 'Now what sort of welcome is that? Actually, I was just about to come, looking for you.'

'How did you get in?' Rachel ran a weary hand across her brow. 'Shaun, I'm tired. Please go. Whatever Naomi might have said...' She looked at him and her voice was firm. 'I don't want you here.'

'Ah, now, is that any way to treat a guest? Naomi gave me a key especially.' Shaun pulled a face. 'There's no need to look at me like that, I've just come to have a talk with you—'

'I don't want to talk!' Rachel tried not to let her irritation show. 'And you're no guest. I didn't invite you over here.'

'But Naomi did.'

'Look, Shaun, I'm tired of saying the same thing over and over. Why won't you listen and just do as I ask?'

'Is it so terrible that I should want to see you?' The phone could be heard ringing the in the hallway at that moment. Rachel glanced towards the door. 'You can't just dismiss me like this.' Shaun rose from the chair and crossed the kitchen. 'I won't let you!' Rachel caught the whiff of alcohol on his breath as he came close, and for the first time she felt just a little afraid.

'Shaun, why don't you do the sensible thing and leave?' She made an effort and smiled gently. 'You're a nice man. I like you, I do, but you're taking this too hard. We spent some good times together but our relationship was never that serious.'

'Maybe not for you.' He shook his head, and his mouth turned down in petulant manner. 'I've never felt this way about someone before. You don't understand how it feels to be rejected.'

'You don't know that,' Rachel murmured quietly. She sidestepped away from him. 'Look, I'd better answer the phone. It could be something important.'

It was a relief to leave the kitchen, Shaun's presence was beginning to get to her. Alcohol. She shook her head. The poor man must be feeling really bad. He didn't usually drink.

She picked up the receiver. 'Hello?'

'Rachel? How are you?'

She hesitated slightly, listening as a clatter sounded in the kitchen. 'Er…yes…OK.' She was more glad than she ever would admit to hear Jean-Luc's voice on the other end of the line.

'Only OK?' His voice, like his ears, was sharp.

More noise. The smash of a glass. Rachel seriously began to wonder if Shaun was wrecking the place. 'I'm…fine.'

'You don't sound fine. Is something wrong? What was that noise?'

Rachel placed a hand to her head. She wasn't sure she could cope with this gruff interrogation just at the moment.

'Is there someone there with you? I thought all of the staff would have left by now.'

'They have. It's Shaun,' Rachel admitted reluctantly.

'Shaun!' It wasn't difficult to sense Jean-Luc's disapproval. 'I see.'

'Actually, you don't!' Rachel replied crisply. She struggled against her instincts to involve Jean-Luc in something that didn't concern him, but she couldn't help dwelling on the alcohol and Shaun's belligerent attitude and pressed ahead. 'I didn't invite him over, but Naomi gave him a key.'

'Tell him to leave, then.'

'Yes…yes, I will…'

'Has he upset you?'

'No.'

'Are you sure?'

'Look, forget I ever mentioned Shaun,' Rachel replied hurriedly. 'Everything's fine.'

'So you have said. Funny that I don't believe you.' Jean-Luc's voice was clipped.

'It's just that he's feeling a little...upset.'

'*Upset?*' Jean-Luc's emphasis on the word made it clear he was not impressed. 'What is that supposed to mean?'

'He's been...drinking.'

'I'm coming over!'

'No! Jean-Luc!' Rachel placed a hand to her head. 'There's no need! Jean-Luc!' But it was too late. The line had gone dead.

Jean-Luc was more glad than ever that he had chosen to return to England. Imagine the agony of their phone conversation if he had been many hundreds of miles away, unable to rescue her!

He drove at speed, but with great skill. His call had been a precursor to visiting the Grange again to establish that everything was going to plan, to oversee his company's investment. The truth was he needed to see her again, something he had hardly admitted to himself over the last few weeks—until now that was. Jean-Luc pressed his foot on the accelerator, and thought of all the things he was going to do to that swine of a boy-friend of hers...

'Shaun, you really must go.' Rachel picked up his jacket, slung casually over a chair, and held it out to him. There were plates all over the kitchen floor. Rachel glanced down at them. 'What on earth happened?'

'I was getting a glass of water and I sort of stumbled.' Shaun glanced towards the drainer. 'They fell.'

'Please!' Rachel began picking up the broken crockery from the floor. 'Go, Shaun! Jean—I mean, Monsieur

Manoire is coming over and he won't be very pleased
to find you here.'

'Won't he, indeed?' Shaun looked belligerent. 'And
what the hell has it got to do with him, anyway?'

'Please, Shaun, see sense,' Rachel replied wearily.
'You've been drinking, you're not yourself—'

'And if I don't choose to?' He walked towards Rachel.
'You and I have had some good times,' he murmured
thickly. 'How can you forget all that so easily?
Remember that day at the fair? And the weekend by the
sea?'

'Yes, of course I do.' Rachel managed a smile. 'We
did have some good times, but that doesn't change the
fact that it's over now.' She swallowed, determined to
stand her ground as Shaun came a pace closer.

'You are a very beautiful woman.' He reached out and
touched her cheek. 'I was a fool to ever think that you
would be interested in me…' He shook his head. 'One
kiss,' he murmured. 'Just one more kiss…'

'You've been drinking, Shaun. I really don't think this
is a good idea.' Rachel backed away at last, glancing
towards the kitchen door. 'Monsieur Manoire will be
here shortly. He's got things he wants to discuss—'

'So you're willing to give him time, but not me?'
Shaun suddenly looked angry. 'Why? What's he got that
I haven't? Oh, no, don't tell me!' He held up his hand.
'I've seen the way you look at him.' Shaun held his head
in his hands, swaying slightly. 'Christ! I'm making a
fool of myself.'

'There you are correct.' The voice from the doorway
was edged with steel. Rachel looked up in surprised relief, pleased that Jean-Luc had somehow managed to get
here so quickly. 'Rachel, have you or have you not asked
this man to leave the premises?' Jean-Luc strolled casually into the kitchen, his eyes never leaving the other
man's face. 'I suggest you do as Rachel asks,' he added
in crisp tones.

'Or what?' Shaun asked belligerently. 'Threats? Violence? I can't believe you'd risk ruining that very expensive suit!'

'Oh, believe it,' Jean-Luc said forcefully.

'You think you can come in here, playing the big I am!' Drink, it seemed, turned Shaun into a reckless devil. 'I don't have to listen to you, and neither does Rachel.' He put an arm around her shoulder, and pulled her carelessly towards him. 'We're close, we have a re-lationship—'

'Oh, yes?' Jean-Luc's expression hardened. 'And yet she wants you to leave. Take your hands off her!' he ordered.

'Or what?' Shaun swayed slightly, and Rachel took her chance and stepped away from his hold. 'Come on, then!' he added, moving in Jean-Luc's direction. 'You want to fight me, we'll fight.' He swung a fist, narrowly missing the side of Rachel's head. 'Are you listening?' he yelled. 'Come on! Let's see what you're really made of—'

Jean-Luc had hit him even before he had finished the sentence. Rachel gasped, staring in shocked horror, as Shaun staggered backwards under the weight of the blow. There was a crash as a chair fell to the floor, and in the next second there was more violence as Shaun swung clumsily in Jean-Luc's direction.

'Stop it!' Rachel could hardly believe what was taking place. 'Stop it, both of you!' she yelled again, as Jean-Luc grappled with Shaun, manhandling him expertly to-wards the back door.

He pinned him against a kitchen cupboard as Shaun continued to struggle, gripping his shirt around the throat and pressing the full weight of his muscular body against Shaun's wiry frame.

'No more! Do you understand? You leave Rachel alone.' Jean-Luc's accent, in this time of stress, was pro-nounced once again. 'You never, ever show your face

again! Or the consequences will be far more severe than
those you have encountered this evening. Now get out!'
Jean-Luc opened the door and with a disgusted look and
practically threw Shaun outside into the kitchen court-
yard.

Rachel watched, trembling as the door was slammed.

'He will not trouble you again. I know his type, a
bully and a coward.'

Rachel heard Jean-Luc's voice, but she refused to look
up at his face. She couldn't believe all that had just taken
place. She sat on a chair, and covered her face with both
hands. 'How could you?' she whispered. 'How could
you do that?'

'You like being bullied?'

'No.'

'Or terrorised?'

'Now you're being ridiculous!'

'Am I?' Jean-Luc was close. Rachel watched him
crouch before her through splayed fingers. 'I heard you
on the phone. I saw the expression on your face when I
came into the kitchen just now.'

'He had drunk too much. He didn't know what he
was saying.'

'He knew very well.'

Rachel shook her head. 'There was no need for violence!'

'Words seemed to be making little difference.' He
peeled away her fingers from her face and looked deep
into her eyes. 'I wanted to protect you—is that so terrible?'

She might have been fooled then that he really cared.
How easy it would have been to forget the past, the
callousness of his departure. To believe that what he had
said had been the truth. She shook her head again, her
eyes narrowed in something approaching dislike. She refused to do it. How could she? It would be like a betrayal

of all those weeks and months spent crying her heart out.

'I didn't ask for your protection or for your help. I didn't ask for any of this!' she declared shakily. 'You haven't changed, Jean-Luc...' Her voice trembled with intensity. 'Still the same arrogant, impulsive, selfish man you always were!'

She saw the hardening of his dark gaze and knew her words had struck a chord. She heard him mutter something low in French, but it wasn't until Jean-Luc's hands gripped her shoulders and his mouth descended that she understood how much.

His kiss was a punishing reminder of how it had once been between them. Rachel hadn't forgotten—not for a moment—the sensuality of his mouth or the compelling sexuality of his whole body. What she *had* forgotten—or had chosen to forget—was the swiftness of her own desire, her inability to keep her own emotions under control.

His kiss wasn't kind. It certainly didn't invite indifference. His mouth moved with lingering purpose, tasted her, invaded the very heart of her, stripping away her defences and pretences and provoking a response.

And she did respond, despite the years apart and the anger surging within. Maybe *because* of the anger—perhaps that was why Rachel kissed him back with a force that matched his own, why she clung to him, loving and hating him all at the same time.

His lean, strong hands moved with slow purpose, positioning her—pulling her from the chair so that she fell to her knees, like a worshipper before an altar. Jean-Luc held her close, imprisoning her against the strength of his muscled body, and kissed her more deeply, more passionately, until finally, after what seemed like no time at all and an eternity all rolled into one, he broke the connection.

The strength of his desire took him by surprise. Anger had been the catalyst, although deep down he knew that was little more than an excuse. He had felt her passion surging through her trembling body, mingling with his own—fiery, challenging—and their kiss had been a battle—hate and desire all rolled into one. He saw her shock—similar to his own, perhaps, but not so well hidden—sharp and vivid, slashed across her face like a scar.

He had acted so foolishly. What had he been thinking of? Where was the art of self-preservation which had served him so well until now?

Rachel looked deep into his eyes. Her good sense had returned in a moment and she had realised the mistake she had made, but by then it was too late. He seemed unaffected by the encounter, she saw, the only sign of passion a slight quickening of breath, a darkening of his eyes. Certainly there were no signs of agony in his gaze, or regret for years passed without her.

'How dare you!' She pulled free from his hold after a stunned moment, hate clearly visible in her eyes. 'Get out!' she told him tempestuously, her voice shaking. 'Get out!'

'Rachel!'

She glared at him, anger surging through every fibre of her body. 'You heard what I said,' she said through gritted teeth. 'I want you to leave.' Rachel got to her feet and found she could scarcely stand.

'Whatever you may think, I didn't plan for that to happen.'

'And that's supposed to make me feel better, is it?' She held her breath and somehow managed to keep from yelling. Her voice was cold, like ice. She saw its effect. 'You think it's that easy—to save the Grange, to take advantage of me whenever you choose? Do you think I'm even remotely like the foolish, naïve girl who allowed you to do as you wanted?'

'You were never foolish or naïve.'

'It would suit you to say that. I think I was—I *know* I was,' Rachel corrected him. 'Oh, yes!'

'Only where your aunt was concerned.' Jean-Luc's tone was assured. 'Then.'

'Get out,' Rachel repeated quietly. 'I never want to see you again.'

'Unfortunately, we both know that that is not possible.' Dark eyes held her gaze. 'I've decided to take an interest in this project, and I see no reason to change my mind.' His expression was as cold as steel. 'In fact, after this…episode my compulsion has only increased.'

'*Episode?* You call this…this assault an episode?'

'When have I assaulted you—when?' He threw her a vexed look. 'Too easy, Rachel,' Jean-Luc asserted in a chilling voice, 'to make out that you are the injured party in all of this. I kissed you, yes, but I do not recall you screaming to be set free.' His mouth curved provokingly. 'Far from it…'

'How could I ever imagine that I was in love with you?' Rachel's voice was barely a whisper. Her eyes glistened with tears as she looked at the compelling, handsome face. '*How?*'

'It is a mistake that we have both made.' Jean-Luc's eyes glittered. 'Maybe that is why I am here—to correct that mistake.'

Rachel watched as he walked to the door, and knew that her overreaction had only served to make everything a hundred times worse. She had never seen him look that way before—cold and so utterly determined.

It was the determination, she decided, that worried her the most.

CHAPTER FIVE

IT WAS almost three months since Rachel had last set eyes on Jean-Luc. Rachel, brushing the golden strands of her hair, gazed out of her bedroom window and watched as the landscape gardeners laid the last of the turf. The contact between the two of them over the past few months had been minimal and in the form of faxes only. Rachel saw this as a good thing, while at the same time hating every tersely written communication which had printed its way into her home at the lodge.

The summer had been dry and fiercely hot. The work on the Grange had proceeded without a hitch. The building contractor was buoyant about targets being achieved ahead of schedule, no doubt looking forward to a very lucrative bonus.

Rachel placed her brush on her dressing-table, and tugged a T-shirt over her head. The day after tomorrow was the official opening.

How was she going to cope with seeing him again?

'You haven't touched your cognac.'

Jean-Luc glanced across the candle-lit table. Yvette, dressed in a well-cut black dress which left just enough to the imagination, looked alluring. He smiled and raised his glass, conscious that he hadn't contributed as much to the conversation—or, indeed, to the evening—as he should have, given that he had been the one to invite her to dinner.

'I thought perhaps...' Her eyes were dark, her smile alive with possibilities. 'Coffee at my apartment?' she murmured. 'Or yours?'

He debated the wisdom of accepting such an offer. He couldn't deny that he was tempted. Celibacy had never suited him, not that he had ever given it a serious try—not until recently, that was.

The summer had been interminable, hot and dry and far too long. He had chosen to stay in Paris—the old story, working too many hours, immersing himself in business. His gaze fell on Yvette's face. She was lovely, humorous, intelligent, so why, then, did he not want to go to bed with her?

'Yvette—'

She raised a hand to forestall him. 'You aren't interested.' Her smile was brief, just a little cool. 'I won't plead.'

'I wouldn't expect you to.' Jean-Luc's gaze was unflinching. 'You're a very desirable woman. In different circumstances...' He managed a smile, then frowned, annoyed with his own behaviour. 'I've not been particularly good company—forgive me.'

'You have a lot on your mind, I can see that.' The beautifully painted mouth curved slightly. 'How is everything in England, by the way?'

Definitely intelligent, Jean-Luc reminded himself. 'As far as I know—good,' he replied. 'I travel there tomorrow to see for myself.'

'I hope you have a good trip,' Yvette replied. She rose from the table. 'She is a very beautiful young woman,' she added. 'I wish you both well. Although, if things don't work out...' She shook her dark head and smiled. 'Ah! And I said I wouldn't plead. You have a very potent effect on women, Jean-Luc Manoire!' she admonished lightly. 'But, then, no doubt you know that!'

'Not all women.' His expression was serious. He thought of his last conversation with Rachel, and shook his head. 'Not at all...'

'So you've survived then?'

Rachel turned sharply at the sound of Jean-Luc's

voice. Even from this distance his presence affected her. She inhaled raggedly, bent to inspect one of the beautiful coral rose bushes that lined the newly paved walk down to the tennis court and tried to keep her composure.

'I thought you weren't arriving until tomorrow!' She looked up as he came closer, noting the tiredness in his eyes. 'You could have let me know you were arriving a day early.'

'Why?' He thrust both hands into the pockets of his dark business suit and slanted her a cool glance. 'Does it inconvenience you in some way?'

'It might have.' Her voice was cool and crisp. She found her gaze wandering of its own accord over his broad frame. His bronze silk tie had been loosened and the top button of his white shirt was undone, revealing the base of his tanned neck. Rachel found her eyes lingering on the curl of dark hair that was visible and the slight sheen of sweat which indicated that it had been a hot journey from the city.

'Are my rooms ready?'

'Yes. Surprised?' Rachel didn't bother to hide her annoyance. 'Didn't you trust me to have everything ready on time?'

'I've had enough of the city, that's all.' Jean-Luc glanced around at the pleasant surroundings. 'Hot summer afternoons are best spent in the English countryside. The Grange looks extremely elegant now,' he added, viewing the new roof and freshly painted exterior. 'The renovation has gone well, don't you agree?'

'Yes, I suppose it has.'

'You don't sound particularly pleased with the results,' he responded tersely. 'Can't you admit that the whole place is far from the eyesore you imagined? The grounds are looking better than I've ever seen them.'

Rachel shrugged and released a tense breath. She tried not to think of how everything had looked all those years ago when Jean-Luc had been a poor but happy university student. She tried to thrust the pictures of him from her mind, the fascinating mix of forceful, unrelenting sensuality and impulsive ebullience which had taken her breath away.

She risked a glance at his hard expression. He had laughed then, and she had laughed with him...

She gazed at her family home which would, in a few short hours, become a hotel. 'It's...fine,' she murmured. 'If you like that sort of thing.'

'Oh, for goodness' sake, Rachel!' Jean-Luc rasped. 'Why don't you just swallow your pride and admit that everything's gone more smoothly than you could have hoped for? That I've left you alone, as you requested, that I haven't been as interfering as you so patently expected!'

'The only thing I want to say to you,' Rachel muttered unsteadily, 'is that I would escape from this...this situation, given the first opportunity! Even if it meant losing everything I have into the bargain!' she added wildly.

'Well, as no such opportunity now exists,' Jean-Luc replied tersely, 'that is not something we will waste our time discussing!'

A tense silence fell between them. The birdsong in the trees above their heads seemed suddenly very loud and far too cheerful.

'If you've finished haranguing me,' Rachel said, and tried to steady her voice, 'I was just on my way to the tennis courts.'

His dark eyes glanced down appreciatively at Rachel's shapely tanned legs and short white pleated skirt. 'So I gathered. You used to be good. Have you maintained your standard?'

'I'm a little better, if anything,' Rachel replied frostily, refusing to succumb to her more usual modesty. 'I thought I'd practise my service.'

'I see.' She frowned as Jean-Luc reached forward and

removed the carbon-fibre tennis racket from her hands.
'A good one,' he murmured, 'and not dissimilar to the
one in the trunk of my car.'

It took a moment for his words to sink in. 'You...
don't want to play?' Rachel shot him a despairing
glance. 'Surely, the last thing you want to do is to play
tennis after your drive from Paris. Why don't you try
the indoor pool?' she added somewhat desperately. 'It's
quite spectacular.'

The attractive mouth twisted with amusement. 'Sell-
ing the place to me now, Rachel? I'll swim later. At the
moment I cannot think of a better way to rid myself of
the tensions of the week than to do battle with you—
unless, of course, you can't handle a simple game of
tennis?'

'It's hot. I—'

'Chickening out?' Jean-Luc's gaze was direct and uncompromising. 'That's the correct expression, isn't it?'

'I'm doing no such thing!' It was the reply he wanted,
of course. Rachel stared at his arrogant features and felt
like kicking herself as a smile of mocking amusement
transformed his firm, hard mouth.

'Good. Give me five minutes.' He began to turn away.
'Why don't you look upon it as all part of the job?' he
continued, glancing back. 'A task to keep the investor
sweet. It might help to remove that dismayed expression
from your face.'

He kept her waiting, as Rachel had suspected he
would, timing it perfectly so that just when she had decided to follow her instinct for self-preservation and
leave the newly constructed court he appeared, looking
ruggedly handsome in shorts and a white, vest-style top
which revealed broad, tanned shoulders and a distracting
amount of muscular chest.

'Best of three sets?'

'I'm not sure if I've got time for that length of game,'

Rachel announced coolly. 'Maybe we should just have a casual knock-around.'

'Frightened of losing?' Jean-Luc removed a couple of tennis balls from the tube at Rachel's feet and tossed them in her direction. He smiled and the gleam in his brown eyes was mocking and assured. 'You used to be good. I thought you'd relish the idea of hammering the hell out of me.'

'I'm still good!' Rachel rose to the bait, glad of the anger which was beginning to surge through her veins. 'You'll see.'

The trouble was that it mattered too much that she won. Tension made her miss shots she would normally have managed with ease. Jean-Luc showed no mercy and positioning all his returns at acute angles, using all his formidable power on his lethal swinging serve. Rachel found herself running around the court like a scalded rabbit. By the end of the first set she was virtually on her knees.

'You're enjoying this, aren't you?' she gasped as they proceeded to change ends.

'It's good—like a trip down memory lane.' Jean-Luc held out a bottle of mineral water. 'Want some?'

'What I want is an opponent who gives just a little!' Rachel refused to allow herself to be affected by his stunning smile. 'Do you have to play every point like you're on the centre court at Wimbledon?'

'You want me to let you win?' Jean-Luc's expression revealed surprise—clearly the idea had never occurred to him.

'Is it too much to ask that you slow the pace a little? It's extremely hot, and I've got new tennis shoes on and—'

'Excuses?' He seemed genuinely amused. 'You aren't playing particularly well, are you?' He tipped back his head and poured a little of the water over his face. 'I remember you as being better than this—you used to beat me regularly.'

'I taught you how to play!' Rachel responded crisply, working hard not to allow the memories to intrude. 'It was the end of winter and we managed only a few games. You've obviously been practising ever since!'

'Maybe I have.' He smoothed back the strands of wet hair which were falling over his eyes. 'Your service is letting you down. It's far too short.'

'Thank you for telling me that!' Rachel replied sweetly, watching in fascination as some of the droplets of water trickled down the bronzed throat. 'I am aware of the shortcomings of my game, just not able—or inclined—to do anything about them!'

'You're trying to tell me you don't care if you lose?' The dark head shook. 'Underneath that beautiful English rose exterior is steel and determination of immense proportions. You've been fighting to win every point.'

'I've been wasting my time, though, haven't I?' Rachel remarked stiffly. 'You play to annihilate.'

Jean-Luc's eyes transfixed her. 'Pure instinct,' he drawled. 'I find it really is the only way.' He picked up Rachel's racket, stared at it thoughtfully for a second and then looked across at her lightly tanned face. 'So, why don't I give you some tuition?'

'What?' Rachel ran a tongue over dry lips.

'Your problem is your toss. Not nearly high enough, and your body position is all wrong—here, let me show you.' He took hold of her wrist, his large tanned fingers encircling it with gentle insistence, and led her the short distance to the base line before she could even open her mouth to protest. More madness—so restrained in every other part of his life—so sure of the right thing to do. 'Now, hold your racket and the ball as if you were preparing to serve,' he instructed.

'Look, I don't actually need or want you telling me

how to—' He was positioning her body even as she started to speak.

'You should stand more to the side, like this.' In one incredibly easy movement Jean-Luc stepped behind her and, placing his hands over the folds of her tennis skirt, manoeuvred her hips into the correct position. 'Now your shoulders automatically follow suit, you see?' he murmured. 'Change your left foot a little and stand closer to the line.'

She could barely breathe, let alone concentrate on his instructions. Clumsily, Rachel shifted her position, aware of the commanding presence behind her. Her heart lurched painfully in her chest. He was doing this deliberately. Testing her. After their last encounter, he must know how difficult it was for her.

'Now your grip.' His right hand changed position, sliding unnecessarily down the bare skin of her arm and halting at her fingers, which were clenched tightly around the towelling grip of the handle. 'You're too tense,' Jean-Luc murmured. 'Loosen up a little.' His words were little more than a whisper against her cheek. 'This is how the swing should feel, like this...nice and easy.'

He demonstrated, and Rachel's heart pounded as he took her through the movement. His body moulded itself against hers so that she could feel his masculine hardness, and was aware with every fibre of her being of his strength and uncompromising power as he guided her arm in the correct way, moving with her so that she could feel the way it should be.

'Now, once more.' His voice was low as he repeated the movement, intent, it seemed, on continuing the agony. 'Doesn't that feel better? More natural?'

Natural? Oh, yes! That was the problem. Having him so close, feeling his body against hers felt so wonderfully right that she couldn't think of anything else.

'You should look towards the net,' Jean-Luc announced softly, 'not at me.'

Rachel could endure no more. She finally found the will-power to pull away but, with a casualness that was arrogance itself, Jean-Luc moved his left hand from her hip to cover the fingers that were clasping the fluorescent yellow tennis ball at her side, and in one, shocking movement he effectively held her prisoner.

'I don't want help with my service! I don't want help with anything!' The breathless announcement revealed more than she wanted, but Rachel was beyond caring. 'Let me go!'

'And if I don't?'

'*What?* Rachel closed her eyes in despair, glad that Jean-Luc couldn't see her face, wishing desperately that the husky French drawl didn't have such a devastating effect on her.

'I may not want to release you,' he continued smoothly. 'What happens then?' She felt the warmth of his breath as he lowered his head and stiffened as the sensuous brush of his lips made contact with the smooth arc of her neck. 'You smell as you always did,' he murmured huskily. 'Honeysuckle and apple blossom, mixed with the moisture of your skin.' His mouth lingered and Rachel felt an incredible ache of awareness deep in the pit of her stomach as he gently ran his tongue along the edge of her bare shoulder.

'Don't!' She swallowed with difficulty, her brow drawn into a fierce frown. 'You're not being fair!'

'*Fair?*' She heard the edge in his voice. 'What has fair got to do with it?'

'This is all a...a detestable ego trip, isn't it?' Rachel asserted shakily. 'You're here to prove some kind of sadistic point!'

'And why would I want to do that?' Jean-Luc's voice was calm, belying the passionate intensity in his eyes as he spun Rachel toward him. 'Do you really believe that

I need to prove a point when the obvious is staring both of us in the face?'

'The obvious?' Rachel didn't bother to mask the hate in her eyes. 'What? That I can't stand the sight of you? That I'll never accept any situation that is remotely connected with you?' she snapped. 'You think I'll eventually come to terms with your involvement in my life? That I'll take your interfering manipulation lying down?'

Broad shoulders were raised in an uncaring shrug. 'Standing up, lying down...' Jean-Luc's eyes glittered dangerously. 'Where is the difference?'

'You can't treat me this way!'

'No? And what about the way you treated me, eh? You and your aunt—so refined, so keen to remind me of my position!'

'I don't know what you're talking about—'

'No, it would suit you to forget, wouldn't it?'

Rachel's blue eyes glistened. 'I never thought you could be this cruel!'

'*Cruel?* Haven't I just saved your precious Grange for you?' He uttered an expletive and then a tirade of unintelligible French, sharp and explosive beneath his breath, and all at once his mouth was descending and Rachel reeled under the dynamic force of his kiss. It was a passionate onslaught that both stunned and aroused her. She was locked in an embrace which tested all of her powers of immunity.

She tried, oh, how she tried, to resist the overwhelming intensity, but it was impossible not to be affected by the strong, tormenting hands, the lean hard frame, the searching sensuality of his mouth.

He had once been everything to her. She had never forgotten how it had felt to be held by him, so tender, so caring, so passionate. All that was lost, gone for ever. There would only ever be this...this compulsive, punishing intensity.

She tried to stifle the sob that rose in her throat, but

couldn't. Jean-Luc lifted his head and gazed down into Rachel's tense face. His thoughts were impossible to fathom and Rachel didn't even try, but she saw the change—was aware of a flicker of dismay, of disgust and something that looked remarkably like remorse in his expression.

He didn't release her immediately. Rachel quivered as he raised his hand and touched her cheek very gently, very softly. 'Forgive me…' The words were so quiet that she almost wondered if she'd dreamt them. Then the formidable chill returned to Jean-Luc's dark eyes and the moment of unexpected tenderness passed. 'I used to think that I loved you,' he informed her grimly. 'Stupid of me, wasn't it?'

CHAPTER SIX

JEAN-LUC'S hands were sensuous, caressing Rachel's heated skin with slow purpose. She gripped his rugged body, aware of his naked strength, feeling the desire growing within her. He smiled down at her, lowering his dark head and kissing her mouth with lingering assurance. The room was bright and sunny, the sheets white and crisp. 'I love you...' he told her huskily, looking deep into her eyes. 'Always... we must never lose each other again.'

'Aunt Clara loves you now.' Rachel reached up and touched the handsome face. 'You have money. You're rich. Like us. We can be a family together...'

'What about Shaun?' Jean-Luc looked concerned. 'He's my brother, he needs me, too—'

Rachel opened her eyes. It was dark. No sunny room, no crisp, white sheets. No Jean-Luc. She released a long drawn-out breath. The dream had felt so real. And he had been so...loving, like the Jean-Luc of old.

It was warm, stiflingly so. She lay quietly for a moment or two, trying hard to get back to sleep. The window was wide open, but there was no breeze. Rachel glanced at her bedside clock and saw that it was just past midnight. The grand opening of the Grange was today.

She got up and wandered to the window. The moon was up, bright and silvery in a velvet sky. Rachel gazed out at the orchard and the still-overgrown garden of the lodge, and then further afield at the landscaped gardens, the tennis courts tucked away in one corner and the impressive outline of the Grange.

She inhaled deeply. It was so humid. Impossible to sleep now. She peeled off her nightdress and thought about a shower. Then another idea struck her—an infinitely better way of ridding herself of all this nervous tension.

Rachel rummaged in her wardrobe, found the items she was looking for and headed toward the Grange.

The swimming pool had been housed in a carefully crafted extension which blended well with the age and proportions of the house. Rachel slid the skeleton key into the lock of a side door, slipped inside and closed the door quietly behind her. She took off her canvas shoes as she walked past the pristine changing rooms, excited at the prospect of immersing herself in the cool, refreshing water.

The tiles were cold beneath her feet. She walked quietly, glad of the moonlight which cast a silvery sheen, reflecting off the glossy surfaces.

The swimming pool was large and rectangular, with a small Jacuzzi set off to one side. Rachel set down her towel on one of the loungers and slipped off her robe to reveal a well-cut, navy blue swimsuit. She scooped her long flowing hair into a tie at her neck and was just about to enter the water when she realised she was not the only one to think of the idea of a midnight swim.

Jean-Luc surfaced in front of her, his muscular arms gleaming wet. His raised a hand and slicked his dark hair back from his face. 'Rachel!' There was the flicker of a frown, then a brief smile. 'It seems we think alike.'

'Yes.' Rachel stared down in stupefaction at his handsome face. 'I...I couldn't sleep.'

'No? Neither could I—not that I've tried,' he added with a faint smile. 'I've just finished working on some papers, and this seemed like a good idea.'

'You want to swim alone.' She half turned, unsure of what to do or say—unsure how to behave. He looked so...stunningly handsome. Rachel thought about her dream, felt the pang of desire deep in the pit of her stomach and began to retreat. 'I'll wait... Come back later...'

'There's no need.' He gripped the edge of the pool and levered himself out. Water streamed from his tanned, muscular body. 'Rachel, this is madness. We cannot continue avoiding one another indefinitely.' His smile was gentle in the moonlight. He seemed different, more relaxed, more like the Jean-Luc of old. He glanced back at the water. 'The pool is big enough for both of us, don't you think?'

Rachel followed his gaze. 'Yes...yes, I suppose so,' she murmured.

'So, swim.' He gestured towards the water. 'This place is as much yours as it is mine—more so.'

Rachel, her heart beating fiercely, threw a swift glance at Jean-Luc. Surely it was crazy to stay, but to go... Wouldn't that indicate just how disturbing his presence was to her? Besides, she very much wanted to submerge herself in the still, cool water. She hesitated for a long moment, fighting her conflicting emotions, then executed a neat dive into the cool water before she could change her mind.

It felt good. Rachel realised she should have taken the plunge hours ago—used up some of her anger and misery after the tennis episode, instead of moping about like a tormented soul all afternoon and evening.

She surfaced after a moment, thrust out slim arms and began a length of crawl, keeping her face down in the water and breathing every four strokes, concentrating on swimming as rhythmically and smoothly as possible. She could tumble-turn very well and did so at every end—backwards and forwards, eating up the water as impressively as any county champion. Length after length after length...

Eventually she grew tired and slowed her pace, twisting onto her back to stare up at the complex pattern of diamond-and-hexagon-shaped tiles on the ceiling.

'I had no idea you could swim so well.' Jean-Luc's deep voice held genuine admiration. 'Rachel...' She looked across and saw him watching her, his body immersed in the water and his powerful arms along the gleaming metal rail that surrounded the pool. 'We need to talk.'

She flipped over onto her stomach, and after a moment's hesitation began to swim towards him—breast-stroke this time, long, graceful movements towards the deepest part of the pool.

'This afternoon,' He spoke quietly as she came to a halt a short distance away, treading water gracefully. 'I didn't plan to hurt you. I don't want...' He paused. 'We used to be good friends...'

'More than that.' Rachel's voice was quiet. Her heart was pounding. She wondered if Jean-Luc could hear it.

Dark eyes gleamed in the moonlight. 'Yes... It still means something to me.'

'Does it?' Rachel was becoming breathless—because of so much physical exertion or because of the way Jean-Luc was looking at her she didn't know.

He held out a hand across the water. 'You sound surprised.'

She didn't take it and kept her distance, half-afraid of the intensity of his gaze. 'Do you blame me?'

'I thought the Grange meant something to you,' he asserted gently.

'It does.' Rachel didn't bother to hide her unhappy expression. 'You know it does.' She was tired. She touched Jean-Luc's hand and his fingers curled around hers, drawing her to the water's edge. 'I'm glad it didn't have to be sold,' she murmured, more conscious than she wanted to be of the sudden proximity of his body, of the expanse of smooth, tanned skin. 'But the fact remains that I don't want you here.'

'I left you alone for all of the summer. I imagined, on my return, that we would have been able to cultivate a different kind of relationship.'

'Well, this afternoon surely showed you that that is not possible!' Rachel's voice was taut. She gripped the rail, making sure there was space between the two of them. 'You've changed.' Her voice was quiet. 'The Jean-Luc I remember would never have treated me so...so cruelly!'

'What did I do?' His voice was calm. '*Kiss you?*' His eyes held hers. 'Is that such a crime?'

'Yes! Yes, it is! If you can't see that then you are even more uncaring than I imagined!' Rachel lurched away from the side, conscious of her need to get away from him. There were so many emotions churning up inside her that she couldn't think straight.

Why was he being like this now? Was this yet another subtle way of making her suffer? Of tricking her into thinking that, underneath that assured, arrogant exterior, the Jean-Luc of old still existed even after all these years?

But did she want the old Jean-Luc? Young, passionate and loving he might have been, but all the wonderful moments they had shared had been forfeited the moment he had walked away.

Rachel began to swim in earnest once again, fast, even strokes which took every ounce of energy. She hurt inside, a real, physical ache. *Don't think*! she told herself, as the water skimmed like velvet over her body. *Don't think*!

He should go, leave this place now. Why stay for the opening tomorrow? What was the point? She didn't want him here. He hardly wanted to be here himself. Masochism wasn't his style—at least he had supposed not, but after his behaviour at the tennis court this afternoon he was beginning to reach a different conclusion.

So go, leave this place! he told himself. Return to Paris and the obvious charms of Yvette…

Rachel was in the middle of a length when a surge of unexpected pain gripped her right calf muscle. Startled by the sudden contraction, she let out a sharp cry and clutched her leg instinctively, submerging beneath the water and spluttering as she came back up for air.

'Rachel?' Jean-Luc's deep voice was sharp. She heard him call her name again and then, just as she began to feel the beginnings of real panic, she felt his hands supporting her body as she struggled to cope with the effects of cramp and stay afloat.

She screwed her face up in agony as Jean-Luc held her. 'What is it?' he asked. 'What's wrong?'

'Cramp!' she spluttered. 'In my leg!'

He took swift action, scooping up her body and swimming with it towards the water's edge, where he lifted her from the pool with effortless ease. Water streamed from their bodies onto the tiled surround.

Once she was safely out of the water, Rachel writhed about on the pool-side, trying to rub life into the muscle. 'Ow! Ow! That hurts!' she complained. 'What can I do? It hurts like crazy!' She yelped as another spasm took her by surprise. 'Ow!'

'Calm down.' Jean-Luc brushed away her ineffectual attempts to help herself and took hold of her foot in one hand, stretching her leg muscle until it was taut and pummelling her calf with strong fingers. 'Any better?' he asked, watching her face for a reaction as he continued to rub the smooth skin of her leg backwards and forwards.

Rachel nodded and released a slow breath, wincing a little at the lingering soreness. 'Yes… I think so…'

'Sure?' A smile curved the corners of Jean-Luc's mouth as the cramp took hold again, causing Rachel to release an involuntary cry of pain and jump around like a lunatic.

He bent over and scooped her into his arms without a word, carrying her over to the elegant sitting area where palms and other exotic plants screened the poolside loungers from the water. 'You'll be more comfortable here.' He sat on the end of the padded seat and lifted her leg across his lap.

'There's no need!' Rachel's voice was breathless. 'I'm sure it will go in a minute.'

'Only if you can get the muscle out of spasm.'

Rachel closed her eyes, conscious of Jean-Luc's near-naked body, more aware than she wanted to be of the fact that her foot was brushing against the taut, flat muscles of his stomach and the low waistband of his dark trunks as he worked hard to relieve her from the agonising cramp.

'This has never happened to me before,' she murmured breathlessly. 'I didn't realise it could be this painful.'

'If I had not been here...' He didn't finish the sentence but continued to rub and stretch her muscle, his face averted from hers in that moment.

'It feels better now.' Rachel, unable to bear the agony of such closeness a moment longer, determinedly swung her leg from his lap and lurched to her feet. 'Thank you.'

'Walk up and down for a while—it will help.'

She took a few paces along the cool tiles, relieved that the pain had finally gone. 'Yes, it feels much better,' she said. She glanced across towards Jean-Luc and saw the look in his eyes, the stillness of his magnificent body, and was suddenly aware of the clinging wetness of her swimsuit which revealed every plane, every slender angle of her body.

'Could...could I have my towel, please?' He didn't seem to have heard. 'Jean-Luc...my towel?' She took an uncertain step forward, waiting nervously as he finally reached across to retrieve it from the lounger.

He stood up and came towards her, his eyes intent on

her face, and although Rachel told herself that the most sensible thing to do would be to move away, to halt this thing before it even started, she could not, or would not, deny herself the pleasure and the pain of that moment.

He swung the towel around her shoulders, wrapping it gently around her damp body without a word. They stared at each other for a long moment, mesmerised, transfixed by an unfathomable physical desire and need which seemed to remove all vestiges of rational thought.

'Let me dry you...' Jean-Luc's voice was husky, a compelling cocktail of warmth and desire. He raised his hands and rubbed the soft fabric across her shoulders in a gently massaging motion, moving slowly and carefully across her back and down the length of her arms. 'Warmer now?' The enigmatic eyes had watched her every reaction, revelled in every sharply drawn breath.

Rachel nodded silently. She had no control over her feelings, no control over her destiny, while Jean-Luc chose to look at her thus. Her body ached with longing. She imagined herself taking a step forward, imagined her hands reaching up towards the glistening chest, saw in her mind smooth, pale fingers contrasting sharply with the tanned skin and black curling hair...

'I...I should be getting back...' She spoke the words, but made no move. How was it her brain could see sense yet her body refused to obey? 'I must.' She spoke the last words as if Jean-Luc had made some objection, as if there were some physical restraint being placed upon her, whereas he simply stood before her, tormenting her with his familiar sensuous gaze.

'I'll walk with you.'

'There's no need.' Her voice was breathless.

'I think there is.' His smile was gentle. He picked up his own towel. 'Give me a moment, will you?'

She could have left then, while Jean-Luc changed. Instead, she picked up her towelling robe, draped it around her shoulders and waited for him.

They walked back to the lodge in silence. The night was still thick with heat. The moon slid behind heavy cloud and it grew dark. There was the ominous sound of rumbling overhead. Rachel looked nervously up at the sky and jumped at the sudden flash of brilliant light far out on the horizon.

'Not far now.' Jean-Luc's voice was deep with re-assurance. There was a pause. 'I don't expect the storm will last long,' he added.

'No?' Rachel sounded hopeful. She inhaled a steadying breath and found that there seemed to be precious little oxygen for her to breathe. 'I'm not as bad as I used to be about them,' she murmured. 'I've been training myself.'

'Good.' He took her hand and gave it a reassuring squeeze. 'That's good.'

'I'm nervous about the opening, though.'

'There's no need to be.' Jean-Luc looked down at Rachel. 'I spoke to Colin—he says you've organised everything very well.'

'I did my best.' Rachel glanced towards Jean-Luc's strong profile. 'He's been a great help. He's an excellent worker, very efficient, as you said. I couldn't have done any of it without him.'

'Don't undersell yourself.' Jean-Luc's voice was warm. 'I have great faith in you.'

'You do?' Rachel's voice held surprise. 'Do you really?'

'Of course. Why do you think I suggested you take all this on in the first place?'

'I...I don't know. I thought you were just being...'

'Just being what?' Jean-Luc stopped and caught hold of Rachel's hand. 'Unkind?' His dark head shook. 'Do you really believe I hate you that much?'

'Not hate...' Her voice was small. 'Dislike, maybe.'

'I won't deny that I have not handled seeing you again particularly well.' Jean-Luc's assertion was tinged with a huskiness which Rachel found particularly heart-stirring. 'But as for hate or dislike…' He lifted her hand and pressed it to his lips. 'Neither is true.'

Rachel felt a swift shaft of desire electrify her body. 'I do want the Grange to be a success…despite…well, everything,' she whispered.

'My involvement, you mean?'

'Anyone else,' Rachel said, a sudden need to be honest overriding all other considerations. 'And it wouldn't have been so difficult. Anyone else…' Her voice trailed away miserably into the darkness.

'You think Aunt Clara will be turning in her grave?' Jean-Luc's voice held no trace of sarcasm but, even so, Rachel pulled her hand free from his hold. 'Or do you object to my help for another reason?' he added, his voice fractionally harder now. Rachel didn't reply, and he added softly, 'I came here to help you. Why can't you believe that?'

A loud rumble of thunder sounded overhead. Rachel flinched and increased her pace, wrapping her robe close around her body, her footsteps more urgent as the first large drops of rain began to fall. She felt more confused than ever. Did he honestly believe that his intervention should have little or no effect on her?

He'd said he hadn't handled seeing her particularly well—how did he imagine she felt? Did he really not understand just how much she had loved him, how devastating his rejection of her had been? Did the past really matter so little to him?

His next words confirmed what she suspected. 'Surely we are both adult enough to put the past behind us?'

'Easy to say.' Rachel couldn't keep the bitterness from her voice.

'You think so?' He took hold of her arm and spun her around to face him. 'You honestly believe that this is—?'

'It matters a lot to you, doesn't it?' she said quietly.

'What?'

'Money.'

A flash of lightning revealed the creamy stone lodge. A thankful Rachel pushed open the small wooden gate which led into the orchard and hurried down the moss-covered path toward the front door.

Jean-Luc followed her into the hallway. The rain was falling harder now, splattering the greenery outside the front door and bouncing against the windows. He closed the door against the stormy night. 'Rachel, have you not been listening to a word I have been saying?' His gaze was steadfast, challenging.

'Oh, I've been listening!' she asserted tautly, flinching as the thunder crashed overhead. 'I'm just not convinced that you mean what you say, that's all!'

'You think I *like* the way things have turned out between us?' He caught hold of Rachel's arm. 'Look at me!' he commanded. 'Do I appear to be a happy man?' He was angry suddenly. Dark eyes flashed fire. 'Well?' he persisted, when Rachel didn't reply. 'At the tennis court, do you imagine I *wanted* to do that to myself— to either of us?'

'Why, then?'

'Are you really so dense?' he asked sharply.

Rachel dragged her arm away. 'Maybe I am!' she replied. 'Perhaps it's the best way!'

He didn't know how to get through to her. He hated this. Fighting with her was the last thing he wanted to do—the very last thing...

More thunder rumbled, followed almost immediately by another flash of lightning. Rachel gave an involuntary cry of alarm, staring at Jean-Luc, her blue eyes wide with unease, and the need to hold her, to touch her, was more strong than ever.

'It's OK.' His voice was wonderfully deep and reassuring. 'I'm here. I won't leave you.'

'No?' The word was a breathless enquiry on her lips.

There was the sound of thunder, like a thousand heavy guns directly overhead. She flinched and closed her eyes, holding herself rigid as all the old childhood fears reasserted themselves.

'Rachel!' She felt his arms close around her, so warm and strong and reassuring. 'It's OK!' he whispered against her damp hair. 'I'm here.'

And he was. In that moment, all the anger and uncertainties vanished as Jean-Luc held her tightly. Rachel buried her head against his chest and closed her eyes, revelling in the wonder of his protective embrace. She had missed this so much, missed him more than words could convey.

They stayed that way while the storm raged overhead. Rachel didn't move—she didn't want to. Where else was there to go? Who else would know to hold her like this?

He needed all of his strength to take no advantage. When the worst of the storm had died away he drew back from their embrace, and looked down into her face. 'Perhaps you'd better try to get some sleep.' His smile was gentle. 'You have a busy day ahead—remember?'

'Yes.' Rachel's breathing was quick and shallow. She had to force herself to concentrate on what he was saying, to try somehow to forget the way she was feeling.

'Are you all right?'

'I think so...' Her eyes locked with Jean-Luc's and a thousand questions remained unasked. 'Yes, thank you,' she murmured. She raised a shaky hand, holding her forehead as if in a daze for a moment, then she turned towards the stairs, climbing each one as if it were a mountain.

'Will you stay?' Rachel was standing at the top of the stairs, looking down at Jean-Luc. 'I mean,' she added swiftly, so that he shouldn't get the wrong idea, 'the rain. You'll get wet...'

'Stay?' Was she mad? Did she really have no idea how difficult just being in the same room was for him?

His voice when he spoke was surprisingly calm. 'Don't worry about me. You look tired. Sleep now. I'll see you in the morning.'

It took ages to settle. Her new double bed seemed too large, and too empty. Jean-Luc paced the living room, glass in hand. He hoped that a little alcohol might help to nullify the desire which was consuming his body. He glanced up at the ceiling. Why couldn't she keep still? Every turn, every squeaking floorboard...

He went into the kitchen when it became more bearable and stood before the window, watching the rain as it coursed down the glass. The noise of the storm was greater in here. Jean-Luc remained where he was until he was certain that Rachel had gone to sleep.

She woke early to brilliant skies. The air had a fresh, clean quality about it, which hadn't been apparent for days. Rachel leaned her elbows on the stone window-sill in her bedroom and looked across at the Grange. It looked perfect in the morning sunshine—better than she had ever seen it.

She thought of Jean-Luc, of the agonies of last night, her mouth curving into a hesitant smile. It was better between them, wasn't it? She hadn't imagined the way he had held her, comforted her? It was tempting to be completely fooled, of course. Rachel inhaled a breath of crisp, morning air. Better not to think too deeply—she would only end up fooling herself all over again.

Thank goodness it was a lovely day. At least the arrangements for the opening wouldn't be in jeopardy. She slipped on a cotton robe in pale blue, thrust her feet into towelling slippers and went downstairs to make herself a cup of coffee.

She really hadn't expected him to still be there, despite her invitation last night to stay. But he was. Rachel ventured hesitantly towards the sofa, her eyes ranging over Jean-Luc's sleeping body. His eyes were closed, and his dark hair, ruffled from sleep, had fallen across his forehead. He looked so relaxed, so handsome, so...gorgeously vulnerable. As different from the autocratic businessman in this moment as night was from day.

She took a step closer. The casual clothes—dark jogging bottoms and pristine white polo shirt—which Jean-Luc had slipped on after his swim, only helped to perpetuate the myth that this was the same young man who had taken her heart with the solemn promise that he would look after it always.

This moment was precious. She had seen him sleep only once before. Rachel allowed the memory, locked away for so long, to resurface. He had been working particularly hard, she remembered.

The head gardener, a blunt, rather aggressive man, dead these past couple of years, had pushed Jean-Luc to the limit, giving him enough physical work for two men and insisting that he completed task after task, even though sometimes it meant Jean-Luc hadn't finished until well into the early hours of the evening. After a couple of months the early-morning rendezvous and snatched meetings, coupled with the constant demanding work, had taken its toll.

They had spent the evening in the lodge, in this very room...candles, food, a warm fire... Rachel remembered the smell of wood smoke, the feel of the cushions beneath her body, the aroma of Jean-Luc's freshly washed skin, the taste of him... She had been talking quietly about nothing in particular, dreams for them both most probably, staring into the flickering flames, her voice soft and sweet, full of love...

She had spoken his name and, receiving no reply, had looked into his strong, handsome face and discovered that he had fallen asleep—eyes closed, thick, dark lashes brushing his cheek, hands resting on her skin, head heavy against her shoulder...

'Rachel…?' His voice was still thick with sleep. Startled, she dragged her thoughts back to the present, marvelling at how little things seemed to have changed in that moment, as sleepy ebony eyes looked up and held her face.

'Sorry! I…I didn't mean to wake you.'

He sat up, rubbing a hand across his unshaven jaw. 'What time is it?'

'It's early…just after five-thirty.'

'*Five-thirty?*' He smiled. 'No wonder I feel like I've hardly had any sleep.'

'The sun woke me.' Rachel glanced towards the window. 'It's a lovely day outside. You stayed,' she added unnecessarily.

'Yes.' Jean-Luc dragged a hand through his tousled hair. 'Do you mind?'

'No! No, of course I don't mind. I…just didn't expect you to, that's all.' Rachel glanced toward the kitchen. 'Would you like some coffee?'

'Yes, thanks.' Jean-Luc smiled. 'Milk, no sugar.'

He followed her into the kitchen after a moment and leaned nonchalantly against the refrigerator, watching as Rachel concentrated on grinding fresh beans and filling the percolator with water. 'The storm did us a lot of favours.'

'It did?' Rachel glanced across, thinking about the way he had held her last night. 'How?'

'It is a beautiful day. It would have been unfortunate to have to move the opening indoors, would it not?'

'Oh…yes.' Rachel heaved a steadying breath. His presence in the small, confined space of the kitchen was disorientating. For a moment she had imagined…well, imagined too much.

Rachel pulled cups from a shelf. This was no good. She had to drag herself back to the reality of their situation. She couldn't allow herself to fall into the trap of self-delusion. Last night had been…it had been like another world, a different dimension. Unreal, with the rain pounding and the thunder crashing overhead, and Jean-Luc holding her tenderly in his arms.

'You received a copy of the schedule?' She could be businesslike when it suited her—now was the time to show him how much.

'Yes.'

'Shall we take our coffee outside? I've managed to clear a little patio area.' Rachel reached past him and opened the door, without waiting for his reply.

She sat on a little wooden seat, discovered only recently beneath a tangle of ivy, and gazed across at the orchard. This was one of the few positions from which the old chapel could be seen—just a glimpse of the spire and the old stained-glass windows.

'What are you looking at?' Jean-Luc sat beside her, following her gaze.

'Just the chapel,' she murmured. 'I'm glad this part of the estate had been left well alone,' she added. 'It's got a nice feel. Manicured lawns and neat flower beds are all very well, but there's something special about a place when nature has been allowed to take hold.'

'You would hardly know it was there.' Jean-Luc eyed the building steadily. 'I had almost forgotten about it,' he murmured. Almost, but not quite. It would not be wise to think too closely now, to dwell on rain-splattered hair and damp lips...

'Do you remember when we...?' Rachel halted.

'Sheltered from the rain? Yes, I do,' Jean-Luc finished for her in neutral tones. 'Do you spend much time there?'

'No. I used to a lot when I was a child. I always thought—' Rachel stopped abruptly and took a sip of her coffee.

She had played out the usual childish fantasies with her friends, but the one she had always enjoyed the most had involved dressing up in a long, cream evening gown of her aunt's, draping a lace cloth over her head and proudly walking down the aisle of the little church with a bunch of wild flowers in her hands. 'I liked it there,' she added. 'It's such a pretty place.'

'This is pretty, too.' Jean-Luc looked around the brick-paved area at a colourful assortment of late summer flowers which were still in bloom. 'You have a talent.' He reached forward and plucked a sprig of lavender from a nearby bush. 'Smells good.' He held it out to her and Rachel took it from him, crushing the leaves between her fingers to strengthen the aroma.

'Do you remember the hedge you had to plant?' she murmured. 'Old Bertram made you measure the spacing to the exact inch! There must have been over one hundred and fifty plants. You said—' She stopped suddenly, conscious of the trap she had fallen into—of the urgent and almost overwhelming need she had had to share the past.

'I said,' Jean-Luc continued, 'that I never wanted to smell another lavender bush as long as I lived!' Dark eyes speared her face suddenly. 'I was wrong about that,' he added softly. 'Lavender is beautiful... It reminds me of your eyes.' He plucked a long stem, holding it firmly between his fingers.

'Rachel.'

'Yes?'

He searched her face with a frown. What did he want to say? What *could* he say? Little that didn't involve revealing how he felt deep inside. He had missed her *so* much...

He shook his head after a moment. 'It doesn't matter.'

'I must shower and get changed,' she announced suddenly, unable to cope with the memories or the look in Jean-Luc's eyes. 'The flowers are being delivered early, and I want to make sure Naomi's not too flustered about her part in the preparations. She only got back yesterday afternoon from Scotland.'

Rachel sensed Jean-Luc's total lack of interest, but she continued chatting on, regardless. 'I put her in charge of table decoration. She's been a bit quiet since her return. I think she must be nervous about the opening. In the old days she wouldn't have flinched about cooking and serving dinner to thirty or forty people. Now she seems less than enthusiastic about taking on even the most basic of tasks.'

There was a moment of silence, then Jean-Luc said, 'Have you asked her what's wrong?'

'No.' Rachel avoided his gaze. 'No, I thought about it a couple of times, but she's become brusque and unapproachable ever since she returned.'

'Perhaps she wants to retire.'

'*Retire?*' Rachel refused to give the idea credence. 'Not Naomi. She's never been a one for being idle. Besides, she's such a part of this place. No, it's not that. But she does have something on her mind. I expect she'll confide in me soon enough.'

'Maybe she's finally realised who I am.' Jean-Luc met Rachel's gaze. 'It had to happen sooner or later,' he added. 'Shaun's her great-nephew, you say?' Rachel nodded. 'Perhaps he's told her.'

'He doesn't know anything. Certainly not that you and I…' Rachel's voice trailed away.

'They will have spoken about my involvement in the Grange though. He will have mentioned that I am French. Naomi's not that much of a fool—she's perfectly capable of putting two and two together, I imagine.'

'Yes.' Rachel nodded, frowning at the prospect of a difficult explanation. 'I suppose so.'

'It would have been as well to have told her in the beginning. Why didn't you?'

'I don't know. It would have been, well, difficult—on top of everything else.'

'You mean Shaun.' Jean-Luc's tone was disapproving.

'He wrote and apologised for his behaviour,' he re-marked. 'But has he really stopped pestering you?'

Rachel released a breath. The impersonal nature of the fax machine had at least saved her the agony of being interrogated by Jean-Luc over the phone. After several persistent enquiries she had decided to send him a copy of Shaun's apologetic letter in which he berated himself for treating her so badly.

'Yes. I told you, everything's fine as far as Shaun and I are concerned.' She smiled, more to convince a frowning Jean-Luc than for any other reason. 'He really was appalled by his own behaviour. I'm sorry you had to see him like that,' she added. 'He really is a very sweet man.'

'I will take your word for it,' Jean-Luc replied dryly. 'However, I suggest you make sure he keeps his distance in the future.'

'Actually...' Rachel hesitated. 'I've invited him to the opening.'

'You have done what?' Jean-Luc looked at Rachel as if she were mad. 'Has he accepted?'

'Oh, yes.' Rachel lifted her shoulders in a shrug. 'What could I do? He's Naomi's nephew, after all!'

'Naomi! Your Aunt Clara!' Jean-Luc shook his head in disgust. 'I really wouldn't have believed, unless I had witnessed it for myself, the hold they still have over you!'

'*Hold?* They don't have a hold!'

'No?' Dark brows were raised questioningly.

'No!' Rachel replied sharply. 'Absolutely not! Of course it will be difficult for you to fathom why I some-times pause to consider whether my actions will affect other people's feelings or not.'

Jean-Luc frowned. 'Meaning?'

'Nothing. It doesn't matter.' Rachel couldn't face an-other full-blown argument. She picked up her cup and saucer and saw with satisfaction that her hand was barely trembling. 'Now, as I said,' she continued in quieter tones, 'I have a busy day ahead—I really must get on.'

If she'd expected protestations then she was in for a disappointment. Jean-Luc hardly seemed to notice as she rose from the small round wooden table. 'Excuse me,' she murmured, waiting impatiently until he moved his long legs so that she could pass.

Rachel couldn't help glancing back as she entered the kitchen. Jean-Luc looked deep in thought, staring out at the orchard as he drank his coffee, barely conscious that she was no longer around.

Jealousy was a new and unpleasant emotion for him. To state that the mention of Shaun's name irritated him a great deal was a significant understatement. Rachel still felt something for him, that much was obvious. He had supposed their relationship to be at an end after the debacle in the kitchen, but now…he wasn't sure. To presume certain things just because they suited him—that was a danger.

He called to her briefly to say he was leaving and then, without waiting for a reply, let himself out of the lodge and strode across the orchard in the direction of the Grange.

It was a busy morning. Rachel did her best to feel cool and in control, even when things didn't quite go according to plan, and it paid dividends in the long run because she felt quite unusually calm as she pulled on sheer stockings and slipped her feet into cream sling-back shoes which matched perfectly the piping that edged the jacket and neckline of her raspberry silk dress.

Rachel stared at herself in the mirror now that the finishing touches had been applied. The summer suit made her look as good as she had hoped—heaven knew, she had spent long enough searching it out, forced eventually to make a special trip to London to get what she wanted.

In some ways it was difficult to realise that it had cost quite as much as it had. It was a simply styled dress with a scooped neckline, no sleeves and just above knee-length, skimming her figure in all the right places. Exquisite fabric, though, and perfect finishing. Rachel adjusted the fitted jacket a little, turning this way and that to make sure that she looked fine from every angle.

She was becoming more nervous now. She smoothed trembling fingers across and beneath her hair, which she had styled into a twisted knot at the base of her neck, and tried to remember the last time she had made such an effort. Certainly Jean-Luc would have never seen her like this. She inhaled a series of steadying breaths. There was little point in denying the fact *he* was the reason she had gone to so much trouble. Never mind the specially invited guests or the staff or the media. It was all for Jean-Luc—although, after their latest spat, Rachel seriously wondered whether he would even bother to acknowledge her presence.

She walked to her dressing-table and sprayed herself with her usual floral fragrance, then, having picked up her small cream clutch bag, left the house for the journey to the Grange.

CHAPTER SEVEN

'You clearly have a gift for organisation.'

'Thank you.' Rachel surveyed the good-humoured mêlée on the vast expanse of newly laid lawn. 'Everything's gone far better than I could have hoped.' She took a sip of champagne, leaning back against the low wall that edged the terrace at the rear of the house. It was very warm. She wished she had thought to wear a large-brimmed hat like some of the other female guests to protect her face from the sun. She was beginning to wonder if her face matched her dress.

'Luncheon was excellent. I've congratulated Pierre. He told me you helped to choose the menu.'

'I offered some suggestions, that's all,' Rachel murmured. 'He's a marvellous chef. Where did Colin find him?'

'Actually, he was my choice. He's worked in France for all of his career. I persuaded him that now was the time for a change.'

'You're good at that—persuading people to do as you want.' It was a statement of fact, pure and simple. Jean-Luc, Rachel noticed, didn't disagree.

He had chosen to wear a cream linen suit which fitted in perfectly with the summery, celebratory occasion. He looked so handsome, so effortlessly stylish. She noticed the interested looks of the guests as they passed by—the smiles from the women.

'The jazz quartet are quite a find—they add just the right ambience. And I like the circus acts. I've received a great deal of favourable comment.' He paused, watching as a brightly dressed clown juggled an amazingly diverse quantity of objects a few feet away and a sinewy man with skin like leather—naked, except for an over-sized loincloth—bent himself into a variety of positions. Another, ten feet high at least, skirted the periphery on stilts. 'Quite a bizarre collection.' He turned and smiled. 'Your idea?'

'Yes.' She tried not to allow the glow of approval in Jean-Luc's gaze to temper her determination to remain cool and businesslike, but it was difficult. *Very* difficult. She took another sip of champagne, and realised belat-edly that her glass was empty.

'Another?'

'Mmm…please. Something less…' Rachel touched fingers to her heated brow. 'I'm beginning to feel a bit woozy,' she admitted, smiling at the hovering waiter. He handed her a tall glass filled with freshly squeezed or-ange juice, clinking with ice cubes, and she smiled her thanks and drank in silence, her gaze firmly fixed on everyone and everything except Jean-Luc.

After a moment, he reached forward and removed the glass from Rachel's hands, placing it carefully onto the top of the stone wall beside them.

'What are you—?'

'We're going to dance.'

'No.' Rachel shook her head. 'I really don't think… No, Jean-Luc. It's not a good idea.'

'Why not?' His eyes were dark and challenging. 'You've danced with just about every other man here. Why not me?'

'You know why.'

Jean-Luc chose to be dense. 'No. I don't think I do. Rachel…' His eyes were compelling. 'Lighten up a little. You deserve to let your hair down after such a lot of hard work. All the staff are out here enjoying them-selves.' He held out a hand. 'Dance with me, or I might have to take drastic action.'

'Such as what?' An anxious frown creased Rachel's

forehead. She glanced around her at guests who stood nearby. 'Don't tease—please!'

'Who said anything about teasing? If I remember, you are extremely ticklish—just about here I think.'

Rachel gasped as Jean-Luc placed his hands on either side of her waist. 'You wouldn't dare!' she asserted, unintentionally provocative. 'Not with all these people around.'

'Do you want to keep refusing and see?' His hand slid beneath her jacket, across her back and along her side. 'I would say this would be a very good spot for a first try...'

'OK! OK! You win!' Rachel twisted out of range. She looked into his eyes and was breathless suddenly. 'Let's dance, then.'

While the music was upbeat, it was less torturous than she had imagined. After the first few bars Rachel managed to relax, to actually enjoy following Jean-Luc's lead. He was a good dancer. That was something she hadn't realised. They had never danced together. They had never slept a whole night together. They had never done a lot of things.

It was only when the music slowed and the lighthearted twirling stopped and Jean-Luc pulled her close that the real agony began.

'Maybe we've danced enough!' she murmured, beginning to pull away.

He raised a dark brow. '*One* dance?'

'I can't!'

'You can.' He held her lightly but with deliberate emphasis, looking deep into her eyes, his fingers moving to link with hers. 'Like this. It's easy.'

It wasn't. But she managed it somehow, holding herself rigid in his arms and refusing to look into his face, concentrating on the sultry tones of the saxophone as they drifted across the lawn—on anything except the proximity of Jean-Luc.

'Can I go now?' Rachel said once the music had finished. She saw the glint in Jean-Luc's eyes and realised her words had sounded worse than she'd meant them to.

'Of course.' He dropped his hands from her body, standing back to allow her to move away, a shuttered expression on his face. 'You've done your duty.'

'Jean-Luc, I didn't mean...'

He waited, and watched coolly as Rachel floundered, searching for something to say, conscious of her own despair because the last thing she wanted was for them to start fighting again.

'I should mingle.' The tone of his voice sent her emotions plummeting. 'You should, too.' A strange, almost dangerous stillness settled over the two of them, then he turned abruptly and left her standing in the middle of the lawn without a backward glance.

What was wrong with him? He was acting like an imbecile! So she hadn't wanted to dance with him. Did he have to reveal his disappointment so readily?

Jean-Luc forced his mouth into a smile. He had been asked a question by an attractive female journalist and he hadn't a clue what it had been about. '*Pardonnez-moi*,' he murmured in a deliberately accentuated French drawl, 'perhaps you would repeat the question?' Beneath dark glasses his gaze shifted from the journalist's face. Rachel was standing a few feet away, watching him. 'Or,' he added, taking the young woman by the arm and guiding her towards the wooden floor, 'we could dance instead.'

Rachel turned away, forcing herself to concentrate on the conversations which were taking place around her. Her smile was bright and completely false. She felt annoyed because she felt sure Jean-Luc had seen her watching him, and she hadn't wanted to give him that satisfaction.

She excused herself from the group, and wandered away from the crowded lawn.

'Naomi, what's the matter?'

'Nothing.' The old woman wiped at her eyes with the corner of her apron. 'It's nothing. I'm just feeling a bit weepy, that's all.'

'Why?' Rachel crouched down beside Naomi, who was sitting under the shade of a huge cedar tree some distance from the house. 'Is it because of the Grange? I know this is an upheaval, but—'

'It's not that.'

'What is it, then?' Rachel scanned the lined face. 'You've not been yourself since you returned from Scotland. What's troubling you? Do you want to talk about it?'

'About what?' Naomi's tone was defensive. 'There's nothing to talk about!' She paused, looking across the lawn towards the marquee and the Grange behind, her eyes red with weeping. 'I know who he is,' she announced abruptly. 'Shaun told me he was French.' Aged eyes looked piercingly at Rachel's face. 'Why didn't you tell me in the beginning?'

'Because…' Rachel shook her head. 'Oh, Naomi, you know how difficult that time was for me,' she murmured unhappily. 'It was such a shock… I was having trouble coming to terms with it myself.'

'What's he here for?'

'Well…' Rachel hesitated, unsure of the adequacy of her own reply. 'He says he just wants to help but, of course, it's business too. He clearly thinks the Grange is a good investment.' Rachel's blue eyes searched for Jean-Luc's figure and found him, standing in the centre of a group. He was still wearing the dark glasses, which only served to make him appear more glamorous and unattainable, and held a glass in one hand as he talked in a relaxed manner. 'He's a very rich man now.'

'You and he…' The old woman's voice was gruff. 'You haven't spoken, then?'

Rachel frowned. 'What do you mean? Of course we've spoken—'

'No, no! About…you know…the past.'

'No.'

'Well, if you take my advice, you'll leave well alone! You know how badly you suffered last time. What's the point in stirring all that up again? I don't know what your Aunt Clara would have to say about all of this, I'm sure.' Naomi sounded disgruntled. 'Maybe it would have been just as well to let the bank have the house.'

'Oh, Naomi! You don't mean that!'

'Why don't I?' Naomi's expression was stubborn. 'He's here to cause trouble, I know it.'

'What makes you say that?'

'If I'd known who he was… I don't like his tone, treating me like I'm a nobody, downright rude he's been.'

'When?' Rachel's voice was sharp. 'What's he been saying to you?'

'Oh, I don't want to go into it now.' Naomi shook her grey head. 'You know he phoned Shaun and told him not to come, I suppose? No?' Naomi's mouth twisted. 'See? He thinks he can just come back here and ride roughshod over everybody! I'm not happy, that's what I'm saying. And you want to be careful, my girl, or you'll find your heart in pieces—just like last time.'

Rachel gazed across the lawn, her eyes coming to rest again on Jean-Luc. Naomi's words were depressing—a blunt reminder of just how foolish she had become. His presence in her life again after all these years was having a debilitating effect. She was losing her good sense, the art of self-preservation which had managed to get her through all these years of emptiness. He looked so cool and confident.

She didn't want to feel this way about him, not any more, but how could she help it? Every time she talked to him or set eyes on him, or even thought about him…

She wished Naomi hadn't voiced her fears. It only served to make Rachel feel more vulnerable, more afraid of what the future held.

I still love him. The truth couldn't be denied any longer. Odd that she should admit it now, with Naomi's dire warnings ringing in her ears, but perhaps that just served to show the strength of her feelings. Rachel gripped the back of the bench on which Naomi was sitting. There had never been a moment, not since they'd first met when she hadn't loved him, every minute, every heartbeat… Always.

She heard the waitressing staff, hired just for the occasion, talking about him later that afternoon. The guests had taken their leave and the circus acts were changing back into everyday citizens in one of the downstairs cloakrooms, while the band was packing up its instruments. Other staff were rushing around with plastic bin liners and trays, clearing away the debris so that the Grange would be ready for the arrival of its first overnight guests the following day.

'Isn't he the most delectable man you've ever set eyes on?'

'And French, too!'

'I wish he had more of an accent. You can hear just a tinge of it every now and then but—'

'He's stinking rich—have you seen his car? Mind you, I wouldn't say no, even if he was as poor as a church mouse. Have you seen that body? He took off his jacket earlier this afternoon—right next to me, he was, and he caught me having a good old stare. Cor, I was that embarrassed! But he was really nice, just smiled—a real sort of sexy grin.'

'Rumour has it that him and her are something of an item.'

'No!'

'Yes. Haven't you seen the way he looks at her? All sort of intense and powerful. They were dancing together earlier, and you could tell there was something going on between them.'

'I don't reckon he'll have much luck there—she's a snooty one, isn't she? Thinks she's a cut above everyone else.'

'Oh, come on, Debbie, she's not that bad! You're just jealous because you've batted your eyelids at him a couple of times and he's totally ignored you!'

'Well, all I wish is he'd look at me like that! Hey! Did I tell you I met this chap…?'

Rachel retreated from the marquee entrance. She had been about to help with the clearing up, but now she decided her efforts would be better directed elsewhere.

'You're in a hurry.'

She spun around and cannoned straight into Jean-Luc. 'I… Well, yes.' Rachel inhaled a deep breath. 'There's lots to do.'

'I think the workforce have everything under control.'

'I'm part of the workforce, too.' Her voice was taut. 'Or have you forgotten?'

His stunning eyes held hers. Rachel couldn't help thinking of the conversation she had just overheard.

'No, I haven't forgotten.'

'What have you been saying to Naomi?'

Jean-Luc's brows drew together in a momentary frown. 'Naomi? Nothing—why?'

'I don't want you upsetting her!' Rachel refused to be convinced by the smooth reply. 'She's an old woman. She deserves a little respect. And you had no right to tell Shaun not to come!'

'His presence would not have been desirable—he has nothing to do with the Grange!'

'He has something to do with Naomi, though—and to me.'

There it was—confirmation that Rachel still had feelings for Shaun. Jean-Luc worked hard at appearing calm,

even though he was being torn apart inside. He resolutely changed the subject.

'So, what exactly has Naomi been saying?' Jean-Luc
looked only mildly interested, certainly not in the least
perturbed, Rachel noticed. 'That I've insulted her?
Threatened her?'

'Don't be ridiculous!' Rachel felt irritation rise. 'I'm
just asking that you treat her with respect, that's all.
She's been with the family a long time. She and Aunt
Clara go back a long way.'

Jean-Luc's mouth curved. 'How could I forget?'

'There's no need for sarcasm!' Rachel was too tired
and weary to keep a check on her temper.

'Has it ever occurred to you that she might want to
cause trouble between the two of us?'

'No!' Rachel threw him a look of annoyance. 'That's
ridiculous!'

'I don't happen to think it is. Have you forgotten how
much she disliked me all those years ago?'

'That's not true! She was just being...'

He looked quizzical. 'Prejudiced?'

'Loyal. Protective.'

'Of what, exactly?'

Rachel didn't answer immediately. 'You should
know.'

'But I don't.' She saw the flash of anger in his eyes.
'Perhaps you'd care to enlighten me.'

'I've said all that I want to say!' Rachel turned away
from him, conscious of the fact that there were probably
six eager pairs of ears tuned in to their conversation on
the other side of the marquee well. 'I've got work to
do.'

'You know, I told myself that I would not allow old
prejudices to get the better of me, to make me angry.
Saving the Grange seemed as good a way as any of
laying to rest the old ghosts.' Jean-Luc caught Rachel's

arm. 'Don't walk away from me,' he said tightly. 'Don't you dare do that to me a second time!'

Rachel frowned, hating the sudden coldness in his eyes. 'I don't know what you mean!' she flared, frightened suddenly by the intensity in his voice. She stared down at his fingers, crushing the fabric of her jacket. 'Let go of me!'

'Don't you think that is what I am trying to do?' His dark eyes transfixed her. 'Or are you really as naïve as you were all those years ago?'

Rachel gulped. She hardly knew what to make of his words. Uttered in the heat of anger, certainly, but did that make them any less intentional—or more so?

Her legs trembled. She felt dazed and perplexed, almost too miserable to think straight. There was a clatter of crockery from the marquee behind. She stiffened, conscious of the whispered chatter of the waitresses, and spoke breathlessly. 'Maybe I am! Naïve! I must be, mustn't I, to put up with your presence here? To even begin to imagine that you might somehow be a changed character!'

'Oh, I'm changed.' Jean-Luc's voice was quiet. 'If there is one thing in this life that is certain, it is that.'

Rachel slipped off her jacket and tossed it over the back of one of the chairs in her office. A former walk-in cupboard, previously filled with unwanted junk, it could hardly be called spacious, but the small window had at least been replaced by a larger one, overlooking the front drive, and it was a place where she could shut the door and escape.

It was late now. The hours since her last upsetting conversation with Jean-Luc had flown—simply because Rachel had worked, without scarcely pausing for breath. She was exhausted, but she'd completed a great deal. When the Grange opened tomorrow at least she'd feel as if everything was under control.

Anyway, it was better to be busy. There was nothing to be gained by dwelling on the unalterable. Rachel had watched the waitresses leave, sharing lifts, piling into a variety of cars—a lively, mixed bunch who laughed and chatted and looked as if they didn't have a care in the world.

'Still here?' Colin, the assistant manager, seconded from another of Jean-Luc's hotels, popped his head around the door. 'You should get some rest. It will be an even busier day tomorrow.'

'Today was bad enough.' Rachel looked up from her desk and smiled. 'I'm going home soon.'

'Happy, living at the lodge?' Colin stepped further into the room. He was a pleasant man with thinning hair and horn-rimmed glasses, fastidious and efficient—a man who knew as much as, if not more than, Rachel about running an hotel.

'Yes.' Rachel thought about her compact home, and the plans she had for a little vegetable garden and a bright yellow guest room. 'It suits me.'

'It must certainly be a novelty after living in a place this size.' He removed his glasses and rubbed his eyes. 'Well, if you don't mind, I think I'll turn in, and you should do the same. Go home soon, and have a good night's sleep.' He left with a smile, closing the door quietly behind him.

Rachel worked on, casting tired eyes over the application forms for the post of resident fitness instructor and lifeguard, which were scattered over her desk. She wished she were at the lodge now, showered and tucked up safely in bed. She was at that stage where she was too tired to work, needing to sleep, but too tired to move and do anything about it.

When the door to the office opened she assumed it was Colin again, who had forgotten to tell her something vital or maybe with more fatherly advice. Busy scribbling a note about a likely applicant, she didn't bother to raise her head but carried on writing with her chin resting on her hand, feeling wearily depressed.

The silence eventually got to her. He wasn't Colin, she thought with a jolt as she raised her head and found herself under Jean-Luc's compelling scrutiny, not him at all...

He was leaning against the far wall—which wasn't so far at all in this most compact of offices. His jacket had been discarded and his shirt was open at the neck, revealing a disturbing amount of tanned chest. His hands were thrust casually into the pockets of his linen trousers.

Rachel's heart skipped a beat, then thudded into life, embarking on a thunderous journey in her chest, as she met his eyes.

'Jean-Luc?'

'This cannot go on.' His voice was dark, full of sensuous power.

'What can't?' she whispered, conscious of the power of his gaze.

He didn't reply. Rachel somehow managed to rise to her feet, confused, hopeful, excited, a little afraid as he rounded the desk toward her. She could feel the heat emanating from his body, could sense the sexual tension and see the desire in his eyes.

It affected her like nothing else could have. In that moment it didn't matter that he was silent and angry and definitely not in love with her.

He wanted her.

He looked at her for a long, long moment. Then his mouth covered hers with possessive intent. He kissed her as if she were the last woman in the world—the only woman. His mouth moved expressively, tasting her, his lean fingers sliding from her waist, across her back, down towards her hips. She could feel every part of his solid, masculine length as he pressed his body against hers, his hands roaming over her body.

'Not here!' His voice was a husky growl. He looked deep into her eyes, so serious, so passionate, so wonderfully French. He held her head in his hands, kissed her mouth with a lingering, sensuous assurance, then took her hand in his and led her from the room.

The Grange was deserted, the creamy stone glowing in the evening light. Their feet crunched noisily on the gravel—urgent, quick steps away from the house and the drive, towards the landscaped gardens and beyond.

Rachel almost stumbled as she tried to keep up with Jean-Luc's stride. He paused as her outstretched arm jerked against his and turned back towards her, tugging her towards his body and holding her in the protective circle of his arms. His mouth slid down to cover her lips in a slow, lingering kiss.

They reached the orchard. Jean-Luc's strong hands manoeuvred Rachel beneath a tree laden with a harvest of crisp, red apples. She felt the roughness of the bark against the bare skin of her arms and gasped as Jean-Luc kissed her neck, her throat, his hands moving with slow purpose over the raspberry-coloured fabric of her dress.

He said not a word—but, then, he didn't have to. She could see the desire in his eyes, the compelling intensity which made him impossible to resist. No man could look at her the way he did, no man could convey such a sense of emphatic intoxication as Jean-Luc did. He wanted her as much as she wanted him, and she was willing to abandon everything if it meant feeling his mouth against her lips, his hands against her skin, the glory of his ultimate possession.

Because she loved him.

CHAPTER EIGHT

THIS was all Jean-Luc had ever wanted—this, just this. Being with Rachel, kissing her, touching her, loving her. He needed her so much... Don't think, he told himself. It frightened him a little—this absolute need. Take it or leave it had been his motto over the past six years—a protective shield of distance and disdain because he hadn't got the one thing, the only woman, he needed in all the world—until now.

He wanted it to be so special. He wanted her to wonder how she had ever survived without his brand of loving. He wanted to forget the past in that moment, to block out the pain of years spent without her. Every touch was designed to bring her to the brink of definitive pleasure and beyond...

Afterwards Rachel clung tightly to him, wrapping her arms around his neck and holding him close, desperate to hold onto the moment.

'Look at me.' Jean-Luc drew away a little and Rachel scanned his rugged, handsome face with wide blue eyes, fighting her uncertainties. She couldn't take any more rejections. If he said something even vaguely critical, mocked or revealed his indifference to the wonderful loving they had just shared then she would be back in her own private hell.

'Nothing's changed...' he murmured. His voice sounded wonderful, so deep and sensuous. He bent and brushed her lips with his own. 'Absolutely nothing...'

He lifted himself from her and rolled over to lie on the grass by her side. Rachel watched him for a while as he stared up at the blue sky overhead, scattered with puffs of white cloud. She repeated his words over and over in her head. *Nothing's changed...* Was that bad or good? He still wanted her, that's what he had meant. He still wanted her as much as he ever had.

She leaned over and kissed his smooth tanned neck, thankful that he wasn't lost to her after all this time.

He turned towards her, smiling gently, but there was a stillness in his eyes, a look that Rachel couldn't quite fathom, that made all her recent certainties begin to feel not so certain after all.

He must have seen her fear for he caught her hand, linking his fingers with hers, and smiled gently. His silence unnerved her. She didn't know what she expected—there had been no time for looking forward, for gauging reactions and responses. Everything had happened so fast—Jean-Luc had always been the sort of man who acted on the moment, but now...

She didn't want him to be kind to her.

'Jean-Luc...?' Her blue eyes were wide, questioning. 'We're going to be all right, aren't we? I mean,' she added swiftly, 'we can start again, put the past behind us. I'm willing...' She smiled self-consciously. 'I'm willing if you are,' she whispered.

He sat up, his broad shoulders hunched over a little as he plucked at some strands of grass. Rachel watched as he dissected them carefully, and she knew with a sinking heart that his body language portrayed more bad signs than good. 'Jean-Luc...?' she ventured.

'Being here... Seeing you...' His voice was dark, full of secrets. He shook his head a little, as if he couldn't quite believe his own actions. A smile twisted his mouth, and he turned to look at her. 'This afternoon...the way we were together... It made me a little crazy...'

'So?' Rachel struggled to keep her voice light. A slow dread was beginning to make itself felt in the pit of her stomach. He looked so intense and brooding. 'I like you that way. Do you remember when—?'

'Don't!' His voice was urgent. A frown creased his forehead. 'No memories, Rachel, please!' Compelling eyes transfixed her. 'I do not want to live in the past. When I think of all the years...' His voice hardened. 'Only now, only for this moment.'

'But—' She opened her mouth to protest. He didn't mean it, surely? They had shared so much, and if she could forgive and forget that which pained her so intensely then surely Jean-Luc could, too?

'I am serious.' His voice held a warning note. 'No mention of how it used to be.'

Silence settled between them. Rachel focused on a point somewhere in the distance, struggling to keep her composure. Their passion had brought all her emotions to the surface. She felt raw and vulnerable, but she mustn't cry and get upset—it wouldn't help. Jean-Luc hadn't totally rejected her—on the contrary, all she had to do was remember that look in his eyes when he had held her, kissed her, made love to her...

'If that's what you want.' Her voice was quiet.

'It is.'

'Shall we go to the lodge?' She forced herself to stay strong. 'I...I could cook us something for supper.'

The warmth of Jean-Luc's smile allayed some of Rachel's rapidly forming fears. 'That will be good,' he replied. He got to his feet and pulled Rachel to hers, kissing her mouth very softly, very gently. 'I don't want to hurt you,' he asserted.

But you might. The unspoken words reverberated around Rachel's head as she looked into the passionate, dark eyes. You might, she told herself.

And then how will I ever be able to love again?

The lodge was welcoming. Rachel had enjoyed playing house over the last few months. It had been pleasant to clean and scrub, to hang curtains and arrange furniture when and where she wanted to. The sweet fragrance of late summer roses, arranged on a rustic, painted table, filled the hallway as they entered. Rachel shut the door and turned to Jean-Luc. 'Would you like a drink?'

He nodded, following Rachel through into the living room. 'I'll cook. You've had a busy day.'

'That would be nice.' He saw her glance, brief and unsure. 'If you don't mind,' she murmured.

'Not at all.' His smile was just a little strained. 'I wouldn't have offered otherwise.'

They were talking to each other like strangers. Rachel walked to an old oak side table and picked up a decanter. It reminded her of that meeting in the drawing room at the Grange, and the shock of seeing him again after so many years. She had felt so...so dazed by his reappearance, which wasn't unlike the way she felt now, but for a different reason.

Rachel closed her eyes. It had been so wonderful to be held by him again, so right. Oh, please! she begged silently. *Don't hurt me all over again. Please! Love me the way I love you!*

She turned with a glass filled with a small measure of whisky and held it out to him.

'You're not drinking?'

'No.' She shook her head, watching as he raised the glass to his lips. 'You didn't used to either. In fact, I remember you used to detest the stuff—'

'Yes.' His reply was terse. Rachel realised belatedly that she had mentioned the unmentionable. 'That was a long time ago. People change. I like this,' he added, changing the subject, and cast observant eyes around the room. 'I like the way you have the house—did I tell you that?'

'I...I don't remember.' Rachel glanced distractedly at the squashy sofa and bowls of fresh flowers dotted around the room, at the books and rugs and cream lampshades. 'Thank you, anyway,' she murmured. 'I'll start preparing the food,' she added, and turned away, unable to stand the politeness of their conversation a moment longer.

'I said I would do it.' Jean-Luc placed his unfinished glass onto a nearby table, catching her hand as she went near. 'Rachel...'

She raised dark lashes, looking up into his face with glistening eyes. 'What?'

He hated to see her this way, but at the moment he didn't have it within him to forgive and forget—not completely. The pain of her dismissal was as raw now as it had always been.

He hesitated for a long moment, searching her tremulous expression. 'I don't regret that we made love, not at all.' Dark eyes scorched her face. 'But this is...difficult...for both of us.' He shook his dark head a little. 'It's going to take time, surely you understand that?' He dropped a kiss onto her lips, then drew back a little. His mouth hovered for a moment, then lowered again, moving with slow sexuality—lighting the flame that was always burning deep within Rachel's body.

She didn't reply. She wanted to say that if she could forgive then surely that was all that mattered, but in that moment all she could think about was the fact that she was in Jean-Luc's arms again, that his mouth was on hers and his hands were caressing her body just as passionately and sensuously as they had done before.

What did he feel? Rachel didn't dare to guess. Jean-Luc had never been one to talk about his emotions so why should she expect him to start now?

They shared the cooking and stood side by side in the neat galley kitchen, washing and chopping mushrooms, and peppers for the risotto they had decided upon.

'I can finish this off.' Jean-Luc lifted a golden strand of hair back from Rachel's face and kissed her ear. 'Why don't you go and have a bath? You look exhausted.' He kissed her again. 'My fault...'

'Who else's?'

Just the action of placing her hand against his chest sent a thrill of desire racing through his body. He would never take her for granted, he knew that. Every look, every touch, would always send his pulses racing, would spark desire and need hour after hour, day after day.

'Go!' He scooped the vegetables into a pan, sizzling with butter, as his desire began to mount. 'I'll call you when supper is ready.'

She half wondered if he might come upstairs to see her. But he didn't, and Rachel tried hard not to be disappointed or to read anything into the fact that while she wanted him desperately, every second, every minute, he apparently didn't feel the same way about her...

He didn't want this just to be about desire. He had to go slowly—a little late in the day maybe, he thought, a curve transforming his mouth into a smile, particularly given the way he had burst into her office, but he could only try...

The supper was cooked to perfection. Jean-Luc had laid a small table for two in front of a small window which overlooked the garden. Rachel, dressed now in a sleek, knitted fawn dress which reached almost to her ankles, padded barefoot across the living room, smiling at the effort which he had so obviously put in.

'Looks good!' She took her seat, watching with loving eyes as he did the same. 'This is something else we've never done together.' She spoke her thought aloud, and glanced across at Jean-Luc's questioning look. 'There are so many things,' she murmured, reddening a little under his scrutiny.

'Yes.' His features were tense.

'I thought...I thought for a time it was perfect,' she murmured, 'but, of course, I was young and—'

'My mistake.' Jean-Luc lifted a jug of water and poured some into Rachel's glass. His voice was taut. 'I was older. I should, in retrospect, have been wiser than to involve you in something you were never comfortable with.'

'If I had known what your intentions were...' She lifted her shoulders in a helpless shrug, struggling all the while to sound calm and composed and as unlike the young girl he had once known as she could be. 'We clearly expected different things out of the relationship.'

'That much was subsequently clear.' Dark eyes pierced her. 'Wrong time, wrong place.'

Rachel frowned. 'You make it sound like...like our relationship was some sort of...of crime.'

'That is the way it was looked upon—at least by some people.' His eyes were enigmatic.

'You're referring to Aunt Clara?'

Jean-Luc shook his head. 'I don't want to go down this path, discussing things that cannot be changed—not now. It's futile.' He picked up his fork and began to eat. She could sense the change in him, the anger bubbling away beneath the surface.

'What did you do—afterwards, I mean?' she ventured quietly. 'Clearly you worked hard to achieve so much in such a short space of time.'

'You're referring to my business?'

Rachel nodded. 'It's a remarkable achievement,' she murmured. 'To have become as successful as you are.'

'There is a certain amount of irony in our situation, don't you think?' Jean-Luc's expression was without humour. 'All those years ago...' His mouth curved into a brief smile. 'I come from a wealthy family,' he continued. 'Extremely wealthy,' he went on, just so that she would be left in no doubt. 'I am an only son. The heir to a fortune.'

'But...' Rachel frowned and shook her head, half smiling as she struggled to accept what Jean-Luc had said. 'I thought—'

'That I was a poor gardener's boy, working his way through university. Yes, I know.'

'But why didn't you...?' Rachel lifted a hand and pushed back the hair from her face, thinking all the while, why didn't you say something?

'To Aunt Clara?' He shook his head. 'To you?'

'But it would have—' Rachel stopped suddenly.

'Made everything all right?' Jean-Luc's voice was heavy with sardonic emphasis. 'Unfortunately, I tend to agree with you. Maybe that is why I preferred to stay poor and unacceptable.'

'You're being unfair!'

He raised a brow. 'You think so?'

'Money doesn't matter to me!'

'No, but your aunt's opinion did!'

'She was my only family—you never understood how difficult it was for me! Please!' Rachel added swiftly. 'Please, Jean-Luc, let's not fight, not now, not after...' She reached out across the table, watching in trepidation until she felt the warmth of his fingers clasping hers. 'I hate it when we fight,' she murmured. 'I hate it.'

'So do I.' His voice was steady, without the emotion so apparent in Rachel's voice but equally believable. 'That is why the past is best left alone. We are wasting time talking about something we cannot change.'

'I know...' Rachel released a shaky breath, gripping his hand as if he were her lifeline. She smiled gently, conscious of the fragility of the moment. 'Any other surprises you want to spring on me?' she murmured lightly, anxious to regain an atmosphere in which their relationship could flourish, rather than be choked with recriminations from the past. 'Maybe now's the time to tell me.'

It had been a joke. She hadn't expected more, but one look at Jean-Luc's expression told her to steel herself for something else. '*What?*' she whispered. 'What is it?' He looked into her face, and she saw the debate raging in his eyes—to tell or not to tell, which was it to be? 'Jean-Luc!' Her voice was sharp. 'Don't do this to me! If you have something to tell me, then do it—please!'

'I have a wife—had,' he corrected swiftly. His voice was low and controlled. 'Our marriage is...' His dark head shook. 'We are divorced.' Should he have told her? Probably not, given the look on her face in this moment. 'I had a wife,' he repeated. 'You don't want to say anything?'

Rachel didn't speak for several long seconds. After a moment she realised she was still holding Jean-Luc's hand, and she pulled away, linking her fingers in her lap, withdrawing into herself as she struggled to come to terms with this startling piece of information.

'What is there to say?' Her voice was surprisingly steady. 'We should eat,' Rachel continued. 'The risotto is getting cold.' She bowed her head, trying valiantly to do the meal justice, but after several attempts she admitted defeat and laid her fork on her plate.

'I thought you were hungry?' Jean-Luc scanned Rachel's face.

'So did I.' She picked up her glass of mineral water and took a sip, meeting the dark gaze. 'I seem to have lost my appetite.'

'You wish I hadn't told you.'

Rachel inhaled a steadying breath. 'Not at all,' she replied stiffly. 'I asked, you told me—despite your assertions about wanting to leave the past behind!' Rachel got up from the table. 'Did you mention it to make me feel...?' She shook her head, lost for words—for ways of explaining how terrible she felt now that she knew that Jean-Luc had had a wife. There were so many questions burning inside of her. So many. 'Do you have children?' she asked quietly.

'No. We were married less than a year.'

A year? A month would have been too long, a week, a day... 'Her name?'

'What has that—?' He exhaled slowly, clearly working hard at retaining his patience. 'Maria,' he replied. 'Her name is Maria.'

'Is she the reason—?' Rachel shook her head. She couldn't bear to know if Maria was the reason he had left her. 'Why didn't you mention this before?' she asked.

'Mention that I had a wife?' Jean-Luc's expression revealed surprise. 'When exactly? For what purpose?'

'If you don't know...' Rachel's voice was taut.

'I married a woman within six months of my departure from England—what does that tell you?'

Strain clenched Rachel's features. 'That you were madly in love?' she replied flatly. Her throat ached with unshed tears.

Jean-Luc rose from the table. He looked formidable suddenly, angry, brooding. His smouldering dark eyes flashed. 'I hurt her,' he asserted roughly. 'Hurt her so much... She didn't deserve any of it. Maria is a beautiful woman, a loving, caring woman...'

'Why are you telling me this?' Rachel asked huskily. She shook her head. 'I don't want to hear it!' Anger scorched through Rachel's body. 'That you can stand there and talk to me about hurting another woman.' She shook her blonde head. 'All those years ago and you could have made it easy for me—for both of us—just by saying who you really were!'

'You share your aunt's view and believe that money makes a person?' His voice held scorn. 'My God! How crazy I was to imagine that once she died her hold over you might have slackened a little! Are you really still as weak and prejudiced as you always were?'

The phone rang, cutting through the tension between them. Rachel stood trembling, staring up into Jean-Luc's face as if in a daze. He had called her *prejudiced*. *Weak*. The phone continued to ring. She watched as Jean-Luc strode over to the side table in the living room and picked up the receiver. 'Yes?'

She pitied the poor person on the other end. Jean-Luc listened for a long moment, then replaced the receiver.

Rachel looked at him. She felt terrible, wanted to cry. 'Who was it?' she asked shakily.

'Colin.' His expression was grave.

'Colin?' Rachel's brows drew together in a frown. 'Why is he calling me here at this hour?'

'It's Naomi...bad news.' He paused long enough for Rachel to prepare herself. 'She's had a stroke.'

It took a moment for the information to sink in. 'Naomi? Oh, no!' Rachel, unable to cope with so many shocks in such a short space of time, sank down onto a nearby chair before her legs gave way completely. 'Is she all right?' she asked quickly. 'How bad is it?'

'Pretty serious.' Jean-Luc held her gaze. 'I think you should go to the hospital.'

He drove her. Rachel sat in silence. It wasn't until Jean-Luc had swung his car into a parking space outside the large, modern building and they had got out of the car that she spoke. 'Has someone contacted Shaun?'

'Yes, Colin was going to do it. Are you OK? I hope you're not about to blame yourself?' Jean-Luc looked keenly into Rachel's face, reading her thoughts. 'She's an old woman,' he continued softly. 'These things happen.'

Rachel wrapped the cardigan she was wearing—an item which matched the long fawn dress—close around her body, like a shield against intruders, conscious of the evening chill.

'I haven't been there for her.' Rachel closed her eyes for a brief moment, summoning all of her strength as they entered the hospital. She considered Naomi's oddly vacant moments, the distraction and irritability. Were there signs beforehand? she wondered. Might she have been acting that way because of what was about to come? 'I've been too wrapped up in other things.'

'You've been busy with the Grange,' Jean-Luc replied.

'And you.' Rachel's voice was flat.

'I'm sorry.' He pulled her to him suddenly, looking down into her face with an intensity that sent shivers of awareness through her body. 'I never meant to say those things.'

'But you did,' she whispered miserably. 'You did.'

Naomi looked old and defenceless as she lay motionless in a side ward. Rachel tried to find a doctor to speak to, but when she eventually did they were reluctant to give details as she wasn't a relative.

Jean-Luc didn't speak when she finally came out from the ward, just rose from his chair and held her in his arms.

'She looks so...' Rachel sniffed, struggling to speak. 'I hate to see her this way—so lifeless. The doctor wouldn't say a great deal—he's waiting for Shaun to arrive—but she doesn't look good. Oh, Jean-Luc, this is terrible! I've only just got over Aunt Clara, and now Naomi...'

'I know, I know.' His voice was deep and soothing. 'But you don't have to go through this alone. I'm here.'

It felt good, hearing those words. And he was. Here. Holding her.

Shaun arrived half an hour later. He looked dishevelled and harassed. A shirt-tail hung out of his denim trousers, and his jacket drooped unevenly from his wiry frame. 'Is she in there?'

'Yes.'

'You've seen her?' Rachel nodded.

'How is she?'

Rachel frowned. 'Not too good.'

'Oh.' Shaun glanced at Jean-Luc and looked away again. 'Well...I suppose I'd better go in.' He opened the door to the room and slipped inside.

'She'll hate being like this,' Shaun murmured, as he gave an anxious Rachel more details about Naomi's condition an hour or so later in the small waiting area off the main ward. 'She'll hate it.' He stretched his arms high above his head and yawned. 'Where's the great macho man?'

'If you mean Jean-Luc, he's gone to get me some coffee,' Rachel replied.

'Why is he here, anyway?'

'We came together. He was with me when I heard the news.'

'I see.' Hazel eyes held hers. 'Naomi told me you and he used to be lovers. It explains a lot.' The bluntness of Shaun's words echoed around the dismal walls that surrounded them.

'She did?' Rachel frowned. 'When?'

'Oh…she mentioned it when I phoned her to say I wouldn't be attending the opening after all.'

'I'm sorry about that,' Rachel murmured. 'It wasn't my idea.'

'No?' He yawned widely, glancing at his watch. 'Maybe it was best, in the circumstances. I know I've acted like a complete fool.' Shaun glanced along the long corridor, watching as Jean-Luc approached with two polystyrene cups. 'She had some harsh things to say about your man there.'

'Naomi?' Rachel frowned.

'Yep!' Shaun got to his feet. 'She sounded odd, actually. Muttering and mumbling on in a weird manner. Not like her usual self at all.' He frowned. 'Perhaps that was the start of it.'

'Her stroke, do you mean?'

He lifted his shoulders in a shrug. 'I don't know. She just seemed different, that's all. Anxious. Upset. I'm going to head back now.'

'Already?' Rachel sounded surprised. 'But you told me the doctors were going to come around again in a little while to assess her situation—to see if there is any improvement.'

'I know, but I can't bear being here another moment. I hate hospitals. Don't look at me like that, Rachel. I'll phone in the morning and find out how she's doing.'

'I just thought…'

'*What?*' Shaun sounded weary. 'What did you think?'

'What's going on?' Jean-Luc handed Rachel her cup of coffee. His voice was deceptively mild as he looked into Shaun's face. 'You're not upsetting Rachel again, I hope?'

'No, I am not!' Shaun met the other man's gaze with open animosity. 'So you can keep your fists to yourself!'

'As I recall, you were the one who threw the first punch,' Jean-Luc murmured. 'Or tried to,' he added smoothly.

'You really do think you're something, don't you?' Shaun snarled. He turned his back on Jean-Luc and looked down at Rachel. 'I'll be in touch,' he told her. He looked as if he'd been about to bend down to kiss her, but straightened, thinking better of it. 'Try not to worry too much,' he added.

'I know what you're thinking,' Rachel murmured wearily, watching as Shaun walked away from them, his figure becoming smaller as he disappeared down the empty corridor.

'You do?' Jean-Luc took a mouthful of coffee.

'You've only seen his worst side. He really didn't used to be so…so disagreeable.'

'I understand him.' Jean-Luc's voice was quiet. 'I was pretty disagreeable not so very long ago.' He drained his cup and threw it into a nearby bin. 'Now, you must go home.'

'No. I should stay.'

'For what purpose?' Jean-Luc asked. 'To sit out here for another hour, and then another? The doctors have already told you there's nothing to be done.' He touched

her face with a gentle hand. 'You are worn out,' he said.
'You need to rest. Tomorrow you can return—early, if
necessary. Rachel,' he added, 'do not be stubborn. You
know I am talking sense.'

'I... OK.' Her shoulders sagged under the weight of
her decision. 'I am tired,' she admitted. She glanced at
her watch, and saw with surprise that it was almost one
in the morning. 'It's been a long day.'

'You don't need to stay.' Rachel turned to Jean-Luc outside the front door of the lodge. 'I'll be all right by
myself.'

'You think I would leave you after all that has happened?' He shook his head. 'I am staying—if necessary
I will sleep on the sofa, but I am staying.'

'There's no need for that.' Rachel's voice was quiet.
'To sleep on the sofa, I mean,' she added.

'Are you sure?' His eyes were still and dark.

'Do I have to beg?' Rachel's voice was sharp. She
felt tired and irritable and unfairly cross all of a sudden.
'Sorry,' she added swiftly, 'that was unnecessary.'

'Perhaps the sofa would be the wisest decision,' Jean-
Luc murmured.

'No!' Rachel shook her head. 'No,' she repeated a
little more softly. She held out her hand, made bold by
her own desperate need to feel the strength of Jean-Luc's
body beside her. 'I don't want to be wise,' she murmured. 'I just want you.'

Slowly, very slowly, Rachel leaned forward, closing
her eyes as her body came into contact with his. She
tilted her face and pressed her lips against his mouth in
a hesitant and fragile kiss. 'I need you, Jean-Luc,' she
repeated.

Almost without being aware of it, she raised her hands
and touched first his face, then his chest, feeling the
powerful, solid frame beneath her fingertips. Her fingers
wandered over his shirt and explored the fresh, crisp

material with shaking hands. She discovered the row of buttons, and unfastened the top two, feeling under the fabric to stroke the warm hair-roughened skin beneath.

She had never been so bold with him before. It had been difficult to keep his emotions in check before, but now... Did she understand what she did to him, how difficult it was to hang onto his control?

Still he kept control. Rachel risked a peep at the rugged features and saw that the dark eyes, fringed with thick, sooty lashes, were tightly closed. More buttons. Soon her pale fingers were dragging at his shirt, splaying out against the bronzed skin.

Why fight it? He knew why. Fear of losing himself, of surrendering the last vestiges of restraint, of loving her too much—like before. Of being hurt all over again...

He lifted her off her feet at that point, a sudden, sensuous movement as his arms swept around her body. He could feel the urgency within her as he carried her up the narrow stairs, and was glad because she so clearly wanted him again as much as he loved and needed her.

CHAPTER NINE

IT WAS late when Rachel awoke. The sun was warm, shining in at her bedroom window onto the crisp white sheets which covered her naked body.

She remembered the night, and a warm glow of pleasure coursed through her body. Jean-Luc had been so tender and loving. He had held her close for a long time afterwards and had been there still when she had woken from a restless sleep, his arms strong and sure around her slender frame.

Rachel turned towards the middle of the bed. He wasn't here now. Her heart turned over in her chest, an anxious frown clouding her expression. Had he left? She was just about to get out of bed and investigate Jean-Luc's whereabouts when he appeared in the doorway, carrying a tray of coffee.

'Good! You are awake!'

'You shouldn't have let me sleep so late!' Rachel smiled and sat up, wrapping the sheet around her naked breasts and feeling ridiculously self-conscious about her nakedness, considering what had occurred the night before. 'There's masses to do.'

'Not at all. I have spoken to Colin this morning, and he understands the situation. You are to take the day off and concentrate on what is important.'

'It's gone nine—I must phone the hospital!'

'Already done.' He set the tray down beside the bed. 'The news is a little more hopeful. Naomi's condition has improved slightly. The hospital say that it is best that she doesn't have visitors until later this evening.' Jean-Luc handed her a cup of steaming coffee.

136

'Oh...' Rachel's smile showed her relief. 'That's wonderful. She might get better?'

'You must not get your hopes up too much,' Jean-Luc warned. 'I do not want to be a damp...' He hesitated, frowning a little as he searched for the right word.

'Squib,' Rachel finished for him.

'Ah, yes, a damp squib,' he continued, dark eyes gleaming. 'She surely has a long way to go before she is properly well again.'

'I know.' Rachel cast blue eyes over Jean-Luc's immaculate figure. 'You're wearing a suit,' she murmured, suddenly frowning. 'Are you...' she hesitated as the realisation that he was dressed for business dawned on her '...going somewhere?'

'I have an important meeting to attend, one that has far-reaching importance for the company.' His voice was steady, without inflection, so that Rachel couldn't gauge whether he regretted being dragged away from her bedside or not. 'Urgent business,' he added. 'I should be back late this evening.'

'That long?' Rachel couldn't keep the disappointment from her voice.

'Twelve hours, maybe a little more.'

'Oh.' She managed a smile. 'Oh, I see.'

'You'd prefer me to stay?' Jean-Luc's gaze was watchful. He had been on the telephone for the past hour, trying to avoid this departure, but circumstances demanded his presence. 'If necessary, I will cancel—'

'No!' Rachel, not wanting to become pathetically dependent, responded vigorously. 'No, of course not. You just didn't mention anything about it last night, that's all. It came as a bit of a surprise to see you looking so...' Her voice trailed away. He looked wonderful, more handsome than ever in the immaculate dark suit, with a white shirt and pale blue silk tie. He had showered and shaved, and his dark, glossy hair, swept back from his face, was still slightly damp. 'You must have been up hours ago,' she murmured. 'You've been back to the Grange for your clothes.'

'The early bird catches the squib.' His eyes sparkled and his mouth twisted into a humorous smile. He leaned forward and kissed her mouth, and she tasted him and was transported back to the wonders of last night. She smelt the expensive scent of his cologne, wanting so much to hold him close and never let him go.

'I promise to be back soon,' he told her.

'It's important, isn't it—this meeting?'

He looked at her, his eyes as powerfully persuasive as always. 'Yes,' he confirmed. 'The company...' He hesitated, clearly not wanting to go into details. 'I employ a great many people,' he continued. 'Unfortunately, I need to be there.'

She still couldn't get used to this sharp, powerful image. Six years before, she could remember him scorning the idea of being trapped by a career.

'There's a whole world out there,' he had told Rachel, 'full of marvellous things to do and see. So many things,' he had said, turning to her with excited eyes. 'We could see them together, you and I. Africa, Australia, the Far East...'

'I've never thought about it.' Rachel had looked at him, her eyes shining at the prospect of visiting new countries with Jean-Luc at her side. 'But, yes,' she'd whispered, 'it sounds like fun.'

'Fun? It would be better than fun—it would be an experience.' His mouth had covered hers then in a long, sensuous kiss. 'One day,' he'd murmured, looking deep into her eyes. 'Soon.'

That had been only a few weeks before the end. She hadn't known it then, of course, hadn't dreamt that he would give up waiting and take off without her.

'You travel a lot now, don't you?' Rachel murmured, drawing back as Jean-Luc ended their embrace.

'Yes.'

'You've seen a lot of the world?'

'Yes. Every continent.' His mouth twisted. 'With the exception of Antarctica. '

'Do you enjoy it?'

'Enjoy?' He frowned slightly. 'Yes, on occasions. Too often, though, it's a chore. More a test of endurance to see how quickly I can get to a destination on time.'

'Even with your own plane and a chauffeur?' Rachel asked.

Jean-Luc smiled. 'Even then.'

'You live a very hectic life, don't you?' she murmured. 'I really have no idea what it's like.'

'I wouldn't wish it on my worst enemy, let alone you,' Jean-Luc replied lightly. 'It's no way to live.'

'Why do you, then?' Rachel asked, conscious in this moment of a need to know. 'Live that way, I mean.'

'Because...' She saw him hesitate, searching for a way to explain. 'Things happen,' he murmured. 'You make decisions, or decisions are made for you...' His voice hardened a little. 'Before you know it you're caught up, living a life that bears no resemblance to the one you first imagined when you were young.' His dark eyes scanned Rachel's face. 'I've changed, Rachel,' he told her. 'You've surely realised that by now.'

'Yes.' She swallowed. 'Yes, I have,' she replied quietly. 'I've changed, too,' she added.

'Have you?' Jean-Luc's gaze was questioning, his gaze intense.

'How could I not have done?' she asked. 'Six years is a long time.'

'Last night it felt like no time at all.' He kissed her mouth gently. 'Phone me if you need me,' he told her firmly. 'I've left my personal number downstairs by the phone.'

'I will.' Rachel's smile held none of her hidden insecurities. 'Have a good trip.'

'You'll be all right?' Jean-Luc didn't seem totally convinced by the face Rachel presented to him.

'Yes,' she said steadily. 'I'll be all right.'

She watched him go as she sat up in bed and sipped her coffee with a nonchalant ease she didn't feel.

He paused at the doorway and looked back, his eyes meeting hers for a brief moment. 'Look after yourself,' he instructed softly, then turned and was gone.

He contacted her late that evening. Rachel, unable to settle all day, was beginning to get a little worried that he hadn't returned. She had thought about phoning his number, and was on the verge of doing so when the telephone rang.

'Rachel?'

A surge of happiness and pleasure rushed through her at the distinctive sound of his voice. 'Jean-Luc!' There was a lot of background noise. Rachel raised her voice, worried that he might not be able to hear her. 'Where are you? I was getting worried.'

'Sorry about the noise—the traffic's very busy. Is everything OK?' he asked.

'Yes. I visited the hospital, but Naomi was resting. They told me she's doing as well as can be expected. The doctors were cautiously optimistic about her outlook.'

'That's good.' He sounded different, a little harassed. 'Rachel...' She sensed the change in his tone. 'Rachel, something has happened. I'm not going to make it back this evening.'

'No?' She waited. Seeing him was what had kept her going through the long hours of the day. 'What is it? Was there a problem with the meeting? Didn't it go well?'

There was an ominous pause. 'I could lie and tell you it's because of business,' Jean-Luc replied, 'but I won't.' There was another pause. Rachel felt a cold dread claw at her heart. 'It's Maria,' he continued. 'I met her father today. He told me…she's not been well. I had no idea.'

'Maria?' Rachel repeated her name even though she knew perfectly well who he meant.

There was another pause. 'Yes, Maria—my ex-wife.'

'Oh…' Rachel's heart thudded painfully in her chest. 'Oh, I see,' she murmured quietly.

'I need to be with her,' Jean-Luc continued. 'To spend some time with her and her family. It's important.'

'I see.'

'You don't have to keep saying that,' he responded softly, 'because I doubt that you do. She is ill, very ill,' he added.

'What's wrong?' Rachel ventured, trying hard to keep her voice level.

'A serious liver complaint.' His voice was brisk, businesslike, masking a whole welter of emotion. 'There are complications, not just on the medical side. Bills to pay… I don't want to go into it now,' he continued. 'You understand, Rachel,' he asked, 'why I must do this?'

'I… Yes,' she whispered. 'Yes, of course.'

'Her family are distraught.'

'She married again?' Rachel asked hopefully.

'No, her parents. When we were married they treated me like the son they never had…' His voice trailed away. Rachel struggled to hear because of the sound of rushing traffic.

'Where are you?' she asked.

'In Paris. I'm on my way to see them now.'

Paris? Rachel inhaled a slow, steadying breath. How easily, she thought, he could distance himself from her.

She tried not to ask, but she couldn't help herself. 'How long do you expect to be away?'

'I don't know.' She heard him inhale. 'This has come at a bad time, I realise that, but it cannot be helped. Rachel…'

'Yes?'

There was a long pause. 'Look after yourself,' he murmured briskly. 'I'll speak to you soon.'

The days passed slowly. He called her, but the conversation was stilted and difficult. There was so much Rachel wanted to say, but she just didn't know where to begin. She asked about Maria, but received only the briefest information in return—the fact that she was doing as well as could be expected and that he needed to stay a little longer.

He asked about Naomi, and Rachel repeated what the doctors had told her—that she was improving slowly. He didn't sense the added tension in her voice when she spoke of Naomi, and she didn't tell him that her visits to the hospital had begun to be an ordeal. It really wasn't something she wanted to burden him with right now because it upset her so, and the last thing she wanted was to break down in tears on the phone, with Jean-Luc hundreds of miles away.

So she kept quiet about the fact that Naomi found her presence more than a little upsetting, and had on more than one occasion burst into uncontrollable weeping at the sight of her. It had got so bad that now the medical staff were saying that it would be best if she stayed away for a few days until the situation settled down.

They ended up speaking about mundane things, things that didn't matter—like the weather, and the fact that the hotel had received a good review in a national newspaper. On one occasion it had become so bad that Rachel had terminated the call within a minute.

Surprisingly, her one solace in all this was working at the Grange. She took great pride in the fact that it was doing exceedingly well. Rooms were booked well in advance, and the reputation of the restaurant and general amenities was high.

Ironically, given the deterioration of their relationship

over previous months, the other person that helped was Shaun. She found herself spending more time with him. He would call by of an evening, after visiting Naomi at the hospital, and give Rachel the update on her progress.

Today they were sitting together, chatting in the hotel restaurant after a pleasant lunch. Shaun seemed more relaxed these days, despite his aunt's illness—the result, he told her, of accepting the fact that there were good things to be had from their newly improved platonic relationship.

'I'm glad you feel that way.' Rachel's smile was warm. 'You know we always got along pretty well. I like us a lot better now that there are no… complications.'

'Except Aunt Naomi, of course.' Shaun released a sigh. 'I know you're upset about the fact that she doesn't want to see you at the moment.'

'It's a bit hard, I must admit.' Rachel frowned. 'I just don't understand why she gets so…emotional when I spend time with her.'

'Perhaps it's just frustration—and you're the one Naomi's decided to take it out on. She keeps on trying to say something to me,' Shaun murmured, taking a sip of coffee. 'The same thing, over and over, and I pretend to understand but I really haven't a clue what she's talking about. I can see the frustration in her eyes. She knows what I'm doing.'

'She was never the sort of woman who could be fooled too easily.' Rachel gazed out of the restaurant window at the landscaped gardens. It was hard to believe that a few months ago the whole area had been little more than a builders' yard. She gave another sigh. She was finding it very difficult to keep her spirits up at the moment. With Jean-Luc gone and Naomi in hospital, her whole world felt as if it had fallen apart.

'You said the talk of eventually moving near to her

sister seemed to cheer her up. I just hope she becomes well enough to get there.'

'It does look more hopeful now, although I received the brochure this morning from the home which has been recommended, and the prices are pretty steep. I don't think Naomi has a lot in the way of savings.'

'I'll pay.' Rachel's voice was firm. 'It's the least I can do. She looked after Aunt Clara for all those years.'

'But, Rachel—' Shaun's smile was gentle '—you haven't got any money.'

'I'll find a way.' She thought of Jean-Luc, and ran a tired hand across her brow. Would he do it? She'd have to ask him. There was no reason why he should refuse her a loan. She'd pay the money off as quickly as she could—with interest, if necessary.

'Missing him, aren't you?'

Rachel decided there was little point in denying it. 'Yes.'

'How long has he been gone now?'

'Four days.'

'Feels like four weeks—right?' Shaun cut himself some more cheese from the board.

Rachel smiled. 'Something like that.'

'I'm surprised he left, what with Naomi being taken ill. Surely you would have preferred it if he'd been around?'

'I suppose I would. But it's a little more complicated than that.'

Shaun raised his brows. 'Oh?'

'He's visiting a friend. A good friend. She's very ill, apparently.'

'She?'

Rachel hesitated. It wasn't difficult to see the conclusions Shaun was jumping to. Heaven knew, in the middle of the night, when she couldn't get to sleep for thinking about Jean-Luc, she had jumped to them, too. 'It's not what you think. He could have lied if he'd wanted to, told me it was just business keeping him away.'

'He is a busy man,' Shaun murmured.

'Yes.' Rachel's voice was miserable. 'Yes, I know.'

'Naomi told me you fell in love with him when you were just a slip of a girl, and he was little more than a lowly peasant boy.'

'I was eighteen.' Rachel shook her head. 'She didn't say that, did she?'

'About Monsieur Manoire being a peasant?' Shaun pulled a face. 'No, I just thought it sounded good. He was a student, though, wasn't he? No money.'

'None that I knew of.' Shaun looked interested. 'His family are wealthy, apparently,' Rachel added. 'I suppose he was rich in those days, but chose not to let people know.'

'Something the very wealthy often do—or so I've been told,' Shaun informed her with a smile. 'Naomi said your aunt grew to have an almost obsessional dislike for him.'

Rachel frowned. 'She told you this—when?'

'Oh…on the morning of the opening. You remember.'

'I think Naomi's been exaggerating rather. Aunt Clara wasn't too keen on me spending time with Jean-Luc, but…' Rachel released a weary breath. 'What else did she say?'

Shaun lifted his shoulders in a casual shrug. 'That you were young. He took advantage. She didn't like him. Your aunt didn't like him. You were too young to know your own mind. That sort of thing. To be honest, I didn't particularly want to know…' He threw Rachel a look.

'Bit like rubbing salt into the wound, hearing about the passionate affair you and he had all those years ago. Actually, she became quite animated at one point, telling me how difficult it was for them both—'.

'Them?'

'Naomi and your beloved Aunt Clara. She said they really couldn't decide what to do for the best.'

'To do?' Rachel frowned. 'They had nothing to do. I know they both of them disapproved of our relationship, but I was determined to go on seeing him whatever happened. What else did she say?'

'Nothing much. I'd given up listening by then. Told her I had to go. You're still in love with him, then? Nothing's changed?' Rachel didn't reply. 'My mistake.' Shaun held up a hand in apology. 'I mustn't pry. Besides, from what Naomi's told me,' he added, 'you've had to endure more than enough prying and interference in your relationship over the years as it is.'

He picked up the cheese board and offered it to Rachel. 'Want some? You know you really ought to eat more. Wasting away isn't going to do anyone any good—least of all you.' Shaun released a sigh as Rachel shook her head. 'By the way, talking of personal belongings—which we weren't—did I leave my watch at your place the other evening? Only I can't find it anywhere, and I'm finding life a real nuisance without it.'

'Your watch?' Rachel shook her head. 'No, not as far as I know. I haven't seen it, anyway. Did you take it off, then?'

'No, the strap must have broken.' Shaun put another piece of cheese into his mouth. 'Could you look out for it for me? It's expensive—a present to myself after a particularly good set of sale figures one month. I'll be so disappointed if I don't find it.'

Rachel smiled. 'Will do. And now I must get back to work.' She rose from the table, leant across and kissed Shaun on the cheek. 'Thanks for having lunch with me.'

'My pleasure.' He grinned, glancing around the swish restaurant. 'I must say I'll be sorry when Monsieur Manoire returns—no more pleasant cups of coffee at the lodge after visiting hours, no more free, expensive lunches.'

'We'll still see each other,' Rachel murmured.

'The only plus will be to see you looking happy again,' Shaun added. 'I'm looking forward to the day when I put a sparkle into a girl's eyes, the way he does with you. Do you think it's something that only French men possess,' he asked teasingly, 'or do all men have the ability?'

'Can't answer that one, I'm afraid,' Rachel replied honestly. 'Jean-Luc's the only man I've ever loved.'

The rest of the day went as slowly as she expected it to. She worked until late, then went back to the lodge and waited all evening for a call from Jean-Luc, which never came.

She debated whether to phone him. She took ages to decide, then did it, and discovered that after all her indecision his mobile phone was switched off.

It didn't feel like a very good omen. Rachel tried not to think the worst, but it was very difficult. Jealous of a sick woman, that's what she was. It didn't make her feel very good about herself, but she couldn't help the mixed emotions that were churning away inside.

Once she had had faith, but that had been thrown back in her face, and now…well, all she knew was it was going to take a reasonable length of time to build it up again, to feel strong and confident in herself. To believe that Jean-Luc really loved her.

She couldn't find Shaun's watch. She looked for a little while in a half-hearted manner, then gave up and went to bed. She hoped, as she closed her eyes, exhausted after a very busy day, that tomorrow would bring Jean-Luc's return.

CHAPTER TEN

'HAVE you seen the state of the tables in the dining room?' Rachel enquired tersely. 'They're a disgrace. I told you so at breakfast and I'm telling you again! Can you make sure the flowers are fresh and the table linen is absolutely clean?

'Also, Pierre...' she turned from the mutinous-looking *maître d'* and focused on the pristine figure of the chef '...I would like you to put in more of an appearance at meal times. The diners appreciate personal attention. It makes them feel special—privileged—goodness knows, they deserve it, considering the prices they're being asked to pay!

'Now, I realise you don't particularly enjoy pandering to strangers, and that your cooking is all you care about,' Rachel added irritably, forestalling the predictably negative reply, 'but just do it, please!'

She turned from the gathered assembly of staff and felt her body trembling a little as she left the kitchens, wondering—no, *knowing* that she had gone over the top and had allowed her tension and tiredness and disappointment to affect her usually reasonable nature.

Halfway through the fifth day of Jean-Luc's absence, this one was already worse than all the rest.

It was her birthday—twenty-five years old today and no one knew or cared. It was silly to feel upset about it at her age, but she had woken up this morning with such unrealistic expectations, rushing down to examine the post, hopeful of at least a card. It would have been nice to receive something personally written by Jean-Luc, something to keep and treasure—the last and only thing

148

she have ever received from him had been the letter, telling her it was all over between them. But there had been nothing—not even a bill to open. Certainly nothing personal for her, nothing from Jean-Luc.

What had she expected? Flowers…ribbons… balloons…? Rachel heaved a sigh. She knew she was being unfair. She wasn't even sure if she had ever told Jean-Luc the date of her birthday, anyway, so how was he supposed to send her something?

Even so, a girl couldn't help wishing…

The receptionist wasn't at her desk when she passed through the large, airy hall a few minutes later, and there were two couples waiting to book in. Rachel smoothed the green silk dress she wore, fixed her best smile of greeting and proceeded to deal with them. She fumed inwardly as the minutes passed and there continued to be no signs of the receptionist, feeling hotter and more annoyed as the reservation book could not be found and the telephone rang persistently throughout the whole irritating ordeal.

'Don't ever leave your post again, without arranging cover!' Rachel snapped when several minutes later the receptionist finally put in an appearance. 'You're experienced enough to know that your presence is vitally important. You are the one person who gives the first, and usually overriding impression of the whole place!' She released an angry breath. 'I cannot believe how many so-called professionals in this building seem able to take their jobs so lightly! I—'

Rachel stopped ranting. Out of the corner of her eye she saw him—unless, of course, she told herself, it was a hallucination because she wanted him to be here so badly.

It wasn't. Her heart leapt. Jean-Luc was walking through the hotel entrance, carrying a leather holdall in one hand and a black briefcase in the other, looking more handsome than she'd remembered.

'Er...that will be all, Carolyn,' she murmured distractedly. 'Just remember what I said in future, OK?'

He stopped and their eyes met and Rachel felt a surge
of feeling so powerful it made her feel faint. It was almost worth having him go away just so that she could
experience the wonder of his return.

Faith—it was all about faith, she told herself.

He looked as stunning as ever. He was casually attired
in a white polo shirt that emphasised his bronzed skin,
with a navy cashmere pullover thrown around his broad
shoulders, matching the colour of his trousers.

Her relief, now that he was back, was palpable. She
wanted to run and throw herself into his arms. She imagined herself doing it, knew that she *would* have done it
six years ago when she was young and carefree, no matter who was around or who saw.

He could sense the tension in her body, the questioning nature of her gaze. Worries about their relationship
had dominated his thoughts while he'd been away—how
best to protect it, to nurture it so that the mistakes of the
past could be put right.

She came to him now, walking sedately, her heels
noisy as she crossed the tiled floor.

'Hello.' Her smile was shy as she stood before him.
She wondered if he had been aware of her angry tirade.
She hoped not. 'You're back.'

'Yes.' His smile was tempered by a slight frown. 'Although for a moment, I wondered if I'd entered a different dimension.' His dark eyes surveyed Rachel's pale
face. 'I've never seen you talk to someone like that before.' He glanced across towards the reception desk.
'Did she really deserve that amount of ill-temper?'

'I...' Rachel struggled to reply. 'No, probably not,'
she murmured. 'I'm sorry.'

'It's not me you should be apologising to,' he replied
evenly.

She glanced back at the girl who was busy answering

the telephone. 'No, of course not. I'll go over in a moment and put things right.'

'You look tired,' Jean-Luc scanned her face. 'Colin said you had been overdoing it.'

'Colin?' Rachel could hardly concentrate as Jean-Luc reached out a hand and touched her cheek. 'You've spoken to him?'

'I called him. I wanted to know how things were progressing.'

'But I tell you that when we talk on the phone,' Rachel replied with a frown. 'I've been keeping you up to date.'

'With the hotel—yes. You said you were fine,' he added quietly, looking deep into her eyes. 'Why didn't you tell me you weren't coping very well?'

'That's what Colin's told you?'

'I've just seen it for myself. That isn't like you,' Jean-Luc added. 'I've never known you to lose your temper over something so trivial.'

'Trivial?' Irritation edged Rachel's voice. 'But she—'

'*Trivial*,' Jean-Luc repeated. His mouth curved into a gentle smile. 'If you carry on in this manner the staff are all going to walk out.'

'Oh, so that's why you returned, is it?' Rachel enquired stiffly. 'To prevent a walk-out? To make sure the company didn't lose some of its precious investment!'

'I returned because of you.' His voice was deep and smooth. 'No one else.'

'Sorry!' Rachel ran a hand across her forehead, which had been aching for most of the long, long morning, hating the fact that he had seen her like this—acting like some screeching harridan. 'I've just been doing my job.' She released a tense breath. 'I've missed you,' she told him quietly.

'And I've missed you, too.' His dark eyes held her gaze. 'It's been a long five days.'

Rachel hesitated. 'How's Maria?' she asked.

'Better.' Jean-Luc's expression revealed his relief. 'She had a transplant some weeks ago and for a while it looked like her body would reject the new organ, but now it's stabilising and everyone is very hopeful.'

'I'm glad.' Rachel smiled gently, wondering about his time in France—what his ex-wife looked like, whether his feelings for her had been rekindled by his visit.

'What about Naomi?' he asked in return.

'Oh…she's doing as well as can be expected.' Rachel thought about the fact that she was going to have to ask him for a loan. 'She's regained a little movement in her arm, but not very much. Her speech is still unintelligible, though.'

'Have you seen her today?'

'No, not today.'

'I'll take you to the hospital later.'

'It's OK. I'm sure you've had your fill of hospitals,' Rachel murmured. 'Actually,' she added, deciding that this was as good a moment as any to tell him about the difficulties, 'I haven't been visiting. She seems to get upset when I'm around. I don't know why, but the doctors said it would be best if I stayed away.'

'Really?' He frowned. 'I'm sorry.' He lowered his head and kissed her, brushing her lips lightly with his own. 'It must be hard for you.'

'Yes, it is.' Rachel's eyes filled with tears. She desperately wanted him to take her in his arms and hold her close.

'It's very busy here.' He picked up his bag. 'If you knew how much I've missed seeing you… I'm going to unpack,' he murmured, smiling lazily, 'then we'll spend some time together.' His mouth twisted into a teasing smile. 'Are you working this afternoon?'

Rachel's blue eyes gleamed. 'I'm sure I can allow myself a little time off,' she murmured softly, looking forward to their time together. 'Do you want the keys to the lodge?' she added. 'I'll get them, they're in my bag.'

'No.' Jean-Luc caught hold of Rachel's arm as she moved towards her office. 'No.' There was a pause as he looked down into her flushed face. 'I've decided to stay at the Grange for the time being. Colin has already arranged a suite for me.'

'At the Grange?' Rachel's voice was small. 'But I...I thought—'

'Rachel, don't look at me like that,' Jean-Luc replied swiftly. 'You must not read more into this than I intend.'

'What do you intend?' She challenged him with her eyes. 'I've never really known, have I?'

'To take things slowly.' He wasn't handling this very well, he knew, but this wasn't the time or the place for an in-depth discussion. 'We'll talk later. I need to freshen up—organise a few things. Give me an hour,' he told her. 'I'll meet you here at four o'clock.'

'But I—'

'Four.' His voice was firm, forestalling any further attempt Rachel might have taken to continue the conversation. 'And bring something warm to wear.'

'Where are we going?'

'You'll see soon enough.'

They had been travelling in his car for over fifteen minutes. Jean-Luc was at the wheel of this different, far more sporty convertible.

Rachel clasped her long hair with one hand so that it wouldn't be swept into a mess by the breeze. She wondered what was going on. 'How many cars *do* you own?' she asked, for something to say. 'Is this new?'

'Not that new, no. I decided to give Emile a well-deserved break.' Jean-Luc turned towards Rachel and smiled. 'You're being remarkably restrained,' he added.

Rachel frowned. 'Restrained?' she repeated. 'What do you mean?'

The attractive mouth widened, revealing a flash of perfect white teeth which looked wonderful against Jean-

Luc's tanned jawline. 'You'll see—in a moment.' He changed down a gear, and negotiated a tight bend in the narrow lane. 'Look! There!' he exclaimed suddenly.

She followed the direction of his arm. It was a field. Newly cut. The grassy stubble, yellow and weak, shocked by the savage blades of a recent harvester. Rachel didn't see anything out of the ordinary. She glanced back at Jean-Luc, frowning questioningly. 'I don't see anything,' she told him.

He manoeuvred the gleaming Mercedes around another tight bend and then across a cattle grid, bringing it to a halt at the edge of the field. 'Now look,' he repeated. 'It is better from here.'

She followed his gaze across the large, flat field and saw a truck and a large wicker basket and something else...a jumble of brightly coloured silks, lying on the ground...

It took a moment for the sight to sink in. 'Oh, no! *Really?*' Rachel turned towards Jean-Luc, her eyes sparkling with delight, her mouth wide and smiling with pleasure.

'*Bon anniversaire!*' He leant toward her and kissed her gently. 'Happy birthday,' he said softly. 'A quarter of a century. How does it feel?'

'Amazing...' She shook her head, her blue eyes held by his velvet gaze. 'Jean-Luc...' Her expression revealed delight. She turned back again as the distinctive roaring sound of the flame inflating the balloon distracted her attention. 'I've always wanted to... How did you know,' she asked him.

'About your birthday? I have a good memory.'

'I told you?' Rachel asked. He nodded. 'And about the balloon?' she added. 'That it's always been an ambition?'

'You mentioned it just once.' He smiled. 'We had only just met. It was early, a misty morning. You were walking, I was cleaning tools, as I remember, and a balloon passed over the Grange and you told me then—I've never forgotten.'

'I don't remember—not about the balloon, anyway. I remember you, though,' she murmured. 'The way you were, lean and tanned. It was so difficult concentrating on anything when you were around.'

'You're pleased with my surprise?'

The change of subject away from the past was obvious, but Rachel didn't mind. 'Oh, I *am*!' Her eyes shone with unexpected tears. 'Thank you,' she whispered, leaning forward and hugging him. 'Thank you so much.'

It took a while for the balloon to become fully inflated, but that didn't matter because Jean-Luc had thought of everything.

Rachel sat on a rug and drank from her champagne glass. The picnic hamper, open between them, was packed with more good food from the Grange kitchen than either of them could possibly eat.

Jean-Luc watched her. He loved her smile. He loved the way she held herself, the mobility of her expression. He loved everything about her...

'*What?*' She saw him watching her.

'Nothing. I just like looking at you. You have a wonderful smile.'

'I love the fact that you've thought of me,' Rachel murmured.

Jean-Luc frowned. 'Don't you think that's what I've been doing while we've been apart?'

'You want to stay at the Grange,' Rachel replied quietly. 'I don't understand why.'

Jean-Luc placed his fluted glass on an empty china plate and caught hold of Rachel's hand. 'We'll still be together—'

'But not all the time.'

'These past few days apart have been difficult, but it's allowed me to focus on our relationship in a way which I could not have done had we been together.'

'You mean you came to the conclusion that you don't want to spend time with me?' Rachel replied swiftly. She looked away. She couldn't help feeling hurt—more than that, she felt a fool for having believed that everything was going to be wonderful just because Jean-Luc had chosen to return.

'*No!*' He caught hold of her hand. 'No,' he repeated. 'Rachel, this time things must be different. I want you—I want both of us to enter into this relationship with our eyes open.'

'My eyes are open,' Rachel told him breathlessly, looking into his face, 'and all I can see is you.'

'Like before?' His dark brows drew together. 'I am a different person now. *You* did that to me. You changed things.'

'*How?*' Rachel's blue eyes narrowed. 'I don't understand!'

He thought about telling her then—making her see what she'd done to him with her rejection, how badly he had been hurt, the devastation... He stopped himself. This was supposed to be a happy day, not a time for recriminations.

He kissed her mouth. 'Let's not talk about this now,' he said. 'The balloon should be ready to go.' He glanced across the field. 'Yes, it is. Now...' He stood up and pulled Rachel to her feet. 'I want you to be happy and enjoy your birthday surprise.'

'Will there be someone with us?'

Jean-Luc looked amused as they walked towards the large multi-coloured balloon. 'I hope so. I may have a talent for many things, but hot-air ballooning does not happen to be one of them!'

'How long will we be in the air?'

'As long as you like—one hour, two, all afternoon, all evening...' He caught her to him suddenly and kissed the slender arch of her throat in a passionate gesture that

took Rachel's breath away. 'This is for you,' he murmured. 'Just for you…'

The flight was everything Rachel could have
wanted—and more. She fell silent as they glided over
the undulating countryside. She gripped the edge of the
basket, looking down happily as a never-ending patch-
work—of fields dotted with cows and sheep, of small
villages with tall church towers and scattered farm build-
ings—opened up before her very eyes.

'You like it?'

Rachel held back her windswept hair from her face
and looked across at Jean-Luc. 'Yes,' she replied simply.
'I do. Oh, look!' She pointed, as eager as a child. 'The
river! Doesn't it look wonderful, glistening in the sunshine? So silvery… And there's the Grange. Goodness,
it looks…magnificent.' Her eyes ranged over the impressive building.

'And the grounds,' she murmured. 'They cover such
a large area. Oh!' Rachel jumped—again—as the pilot
released a valve and flames were sent shooting above
their heads.

Jean-Luc's mouth twisted into a smile. He put an arm
around her waist. 'You just cannot get used to that noise,
can you?'

'How far do you think we've travelled?' Rachel
scanned the three-hundred-and-sixty-degree horizon,
conscious of the trees not far below the basket, firmly
putting the prospect of an eventful landing to the back
of her mind.

'Fifteen, maybe twenty miles.'

'How do we get back?' Rachel asked.

'It's OK. Look down there. No, this way…' Jean-Luc
turned Rachel's body so that it faced in the right direction. 'That truck. It's been following the balloon ever
since we set off. Once we land it will pick us up and
take us back to the car.'

'Oh, of course.' Rachel turned her head, conscious of

his body so close to her own. 'And there was I imagining we'd have a long, hot walk ahead of us,' she murmured lightly.

'It's very beautiful from up here, isn't it?' he observed softly, moving his hands to grip the basket on either side of Rachel's body. He kissed her neck. 'No hustle, no intrusions. Just the sky and the sun and the countryside below... I feel as if I could stay up here for ever,' he added.

'What's happened to the businessman all of a sudden?' she asked. 'The wheeler-dealer who likes to take risks and build up empires?'

'Oh, he's taking a holiday.'

'He needs one.' Rachel twisted around and kissed his tanned cheek. 'I think he works far too hard as it is. Although,' she added a little more seriously, 'I'm not fool enough to believe one that one ride in a hot-air balloon will change anything.'

'You sound hard and cynical.' Jean-Luc's lips brushed her mouth. 'Don't be like that.'

'Is Maria pretty?' The question had flown into Rachel's head, and she asked it, without pausing to think.

'Not now.' Jean-Luc's voice was firm. 'Don't spoil things.'

'I just asked—'

'An extremely pointless question.' Jean-Luc lifted a strand of hair away from Rachel's face. 'What does it matter whether she is pretty or not?'

'I just wondered.' Rachel frowned. 'You're right, I spoke without thinking. It's just...these last few days...'

'You have nothing to worry about.'

'She was your wife—that's a very strong tie.' He didn't deny it, she noticed. 'Can't you imagine what I've been going through?' she added.

'And if I tell you she is dark and beautiful, with a

wonderful smile and a happy disposition, that will help matters, will it?' His tone was blunt.

'Is she?' Rachel's voice was small.

'Is she what?' He sounded a little angry now. 'Yes,' he added distractedly. 'Maria is all of those things.'

Rachel released a steadying breath. 'I'm surprised you ever let her go. She sounds…perfect.'

'Like an angel.'

'You said…you said you hurt her.' Rachel fixed her gaze on the horizon. 'What did you do?'

'It was five years ago.' He spoke quietly. 'I told you I was disagreeable. I married her,' he added simply. 'I shouldn't have. I took her love and treated it with disdain. I did to her…' He paused. His chest rose and fell. He'd almost said, 'what you did to me', but stopped himself just in time. 'Why have you done this?' His dark eyes demanded an answer as he turned Rachel towards him. 'You're spoiling what was supposed to be a happy occasion.'

'I can't help it.' Rachel shook her head. 'I just needed to know—'

'How badly I made a mess of things?' His mouth hardened into a disapproving line. 'Does it make you feel better to realise that when our relationship ended I lost all sense of what was right anymore?'

They had almost forgotten they were not alone. There was a sudden shout of warning from the pilot, and then the balloon dipped unexpectedly, catching the topmost branches of a tree.

Rachel gave a cry of alarm as the basket lost height, and was reassured to feel the strength of Jean-Luc's arm around her waist as the balloon descended the last few feet and landed with a violent thud on the edge of a small field, before being dragged along for a few feet at an alarming angle.

'Are you all right?' Jean-Luc's voice was urgent, full of concern.

Rachel looked up in dazed wonder, releasing a breath. 'I suppose the uncertainty of the landing is all part of the thrill?'

His mouth curved into a smile. 'A thrill I could do without.'

'I'm sorry,' she murmured. 'About before. It's just...' Rachel shook her head. 'I don't *mean* to act this way.'

'We're both guilty of saying and doing things we don't mean,' Jean-Luc murmured. 'That is all part of human nature.'

'So I'm forgiven?' she murmured.

His expression was a tantalising mix of tenderness and passion. 'You are forgiven,' he repeated softly.

Their return journey was completed in record time. Jean-Luc pulled the Mercedes to a halt outside the lodge.

'Are you in the mood for a visitor?' he asked smoothly.

Rachel's voice was deliberately teasing. 'Don't you want to settle in at the Grange?'

'You know what I want.' Jean-Luc's mouth curved into a flirtatious smile. He reached out and touched her face. 'Don't you?'

The lodge felt more like home than the Grange had ever done. Rachel wondered if it was because all the special moments had been spent here with Jean-Luc.

They made love all evening, tender, passionate, intense love. The separation of the past few days had increased Jean-Luc's ardour. His loving was sublime, more incredible than the best that they had ever shared. Rachel clung to him when he held her afterwards, revelling in his masculine touch, in the eroticism of his husky French drawl. He spoke to her with such feeling, words she couldn't and didn't need to understand. Words of love.

It was almost four in the morning. Rachel stirred, moving her limbs across the sheets until they touched the muscular hardness of Jean-Luc's body beside her. She turned towards him and smiled contentedly in her sleep, her hand across his broad chest, pressing herself up close...

Jean-Luc felt her touch. His body was rigid with tension. Not good. He inhaled deeply, trying to regain some of his equilibrium—except, of course, that particular physical and mental state was a pretty difficult acquisition when he was in Rachel's company. No other woman in the world was capable of making him feel so utterly high—or low.

His powerful fingers curled around the object in his right hand, squeezing it until the metal strap bit into his palm. It was Shaun's watch—he could picture it on Shaun's wrist even now as he held it. An expensive, rather ostentatious timepiece which was meant to catch the eye...

Jean-Luc took another deep breath. This surely couldn't be happening to him, could it? That man's watch in Rachel's bedroom? His chest felt tight with anxiety. He understood and accepted the fragility and vulnerability of his reasoning, the fragments of fear about his relationship with Rachel which were embedded like splinters in his mind. Had they...?

Jean-Luc's left hand clenched at his side, thrusting momentarily against the smooth, achingly erotic length of Rachel's inner thigh. He tried to be convinced by any number of plausible scenarios why he should find Shaun's watch beside Rachel's bed, but in his present state of mind all he seemed able to do was to think the worst.

How long had he been lying here, doing just that? He glanced at the luminous dial of the watch in his hand— it was over an hour since he had got up to go to the bathroom and had caught sight of the metal casing, lying on the floor halfway between the bed and the oak side table.

He was tired and yet he had never felt more awake. Colin, of all people, had mentioned Shaun's frequent visits to the hotel in his absence, and Jean-Luc in his euphoria at seeing Rachel again had chosen not to dwell on the information, determined not to think the worst—but now?

Doubt ate away at his soul—a legacy of six years ago when he had had to face the fact that Rachel's involvement and commitment to him hadn't been as intense or complete as he had so desperately wanted and supposed.

She moved against him once more, and Jean-Luc felt the familiar stirrings of sexual desire. She was so lovely in her naked beauty—how could any man resist?

Shaun had turned the situation of Naomi's illness to his advantage, no doubt. Used it to ingratiate himself again, to get close—as close or closer than he had been before?

More torturous images, coupled with fears he'd hardly known he'd possessed, tormented him. Five days he had been gone, and during that time their communication had been aggravatingly dismal but not worryingly so—not until now.

He knew about his own inability to express emotion over the telephone—for him it was and always had been simply a tool of business, but that didn't explain Rachel's own reluctance to talk about anything other than the hotel and day-to-day trivia, did it?

She moved again, her hand sliding across his bare chest and her lips brushing the skin of his arm as she snuggled against him. Jean-Luc worked at keeping still. He ached deep inside. So tense, so full of doubts. He longed to hold her, to bury his face against her silky skin, to feel the suppleness and warmth of her body…

He was awake. Rachel peered into the half-light and watched his profile for a long moment, saw the way he was staring up at the ceiling. This was a wonderful moment, just this—waking up, finding him by her side, feeling the strength of him.

'Can't you sleep?' she murmured throatily. He didn't reply. 'Jean-Luc?' She raised herself up on one arm, lifting her tangle of hair from her face and propping her head with her elbow. 'Is something the matter?' She watched as he sat up. The sheet which had partially covered his torso fell to his waist. Rachel stroked a finger along the rippling planes of his stomach. 'You should have woken me earlier,' she commented lightly. 'I would have kept you company.'

He looked at her, but there was no softening of the finely moulded mouth, no hoped-for gleam in his glorious dark brown eyes. It was almost dawn. Rachel could sense that something was wrong. 'Jean-Luc... ? What is it? Are you unwell?' She sat up, oblivious of her own nakedness as she reached out a hand toward the taut, handsome face.

'Have you been seeing Shaun while I was away?'

'Shaun?' Rachel frowned. Her fingers stilled. She didn't like the tone of his voice. '*Been seeing?*' she repeated.

'That's what I said.' His chest rose and fell very slowly. 'Has he been here?'

'Why do you—?'

'Just answer the question!'

He saw her flinch at the anger in his voice and wished the cool, clear judgement which served him so well as far as business was concerned could be brought into play in this moment. 'It's a simple question,' he added, in more even tones. 'Has he been here?'

Rachel stroked a finger along his hardened jawline. 'Please, Jean-Luc! Don't be like this!'

He caught her hand, his strong fingers curling around her wrist. '*Has he?*'

'No!'

'You lie.' The tone of his voice was flat. He allowed

her hand to fall away. 'Why? Why do you need to do that?'

'OK, then, yes, he has been here, but—'

'So! After the way he treated you?'

'I told you, he wasn't himself then—'

'Did you sleep with him?'

There was silence. She didn't deny it. *Please!* Jean-Luc begged silently. Deny it now—quickly. He looked into her clear, blue eyes and, instead of contrition, simply saw anger.

'What has got into you?' Rachel stared into Jean-Luc's tense face, bemused with sleep, hardly able to comprehend what was going on. 'You...you think...?' She shook her head, her eyes narrowing. 'You don't trust me.'

'I found a watch. I believe it is his.'

'Where?' Rachel asked, almost too dazed to focus on the questions that mattered. 'Where did you find it?'

'At the side of the bed.'

'No, you can't have! We didn't— I mean, he never came in here.'

'I want to believe that.'

'You *want* to?' Rachel exhaled sharply. She lifted her hands to her head and dragged trembling fingers through her hair. 'How long have you been lying there, thinking...? I can't believe we're having this conversation,' she exploded. 'After everything we've been through together—'

'Together?' Jean-Luc's expression was harsh. 'Have you forgotten we've spent the last six years apart?' he said through gritted teeth. 'Where was the togetherness then? I ask you that!'

'I thought...' Rachel frowned, biting down on her bottom lip to prevent herself from crying.

'You thought what?'

'You really don't trust me,' she whispered. 'Will you ever?'

'You saw a great deal of Shaun while I was away, I believe. Yet you never mentioned his name, not once.'

'I didn't think it important.'

'Important enough now that I discover his watch beside your bed. This bed, the place where we—'

'You're tense and angry and tired.' She turned her head so that he couldn't see the tears welling up in her eyes. 'I'm sure you don't mean to be this way—'

'You are making excuses for *my* behaviour?'

'Now you sound arrogant.' Rachel swallowed against the lump in her throat. 'You don't sound like the Jean-Luc I once knew-'

'Maybe because he doesn't exist any more! *Six years!*'

'You don't need to remind me!' A sob caught in Rachel's throat. 'It lies between us like a great wasteland—a void.'

'You have no idea how I felt during that time,' Jean-Luc snarled. 'No idea at all!'

'You married.' Rachel's voice was barely a whisper.

'Yes, I married!' His expression, she saw, was bleak. 'And it ended. Finished before it had begun!'

'You must have loved her.'

'Must I?' He threw her a vexed look. 'Because we exchanged rings and she looked beautiful in a white dress?'

'Did she?' Rachel couldn't help herself.

'What?'

'Look beautiful?'

His eyes glittered. 'Like a princess!'

'I see.'

'No, you don't! If you did...' He released a tense breath. 'Perhaps it was a mistake for me to return,' he said flatly. 'I imagined I would be able to deal with the recriminations, with seeing you again, but it is not that easy—for either of us.'

'What do you mean?' Rachel whispered.

'I think you know what I mean. I want you—so much.

But I cannot forget the past—neither of us can. The pain of it haunts me...' His jaw tightened. 'He was here—in this bedroom. Why deny it?'

'Why, indeed?' Rachel struggled to speak. Her throat was tight and she wanted to cry, but her emotions were locked deep inside. 'You look as if...' She gazed into his eyes and saw the anguish of a man struggling to make a difficult decision. 'You're right, we can't go on like this.' A cold, metallic expression fell across her face.

'We haven't thought this through. Desire, attraction... whatever it is that makes us so...so...' She tried to stay calm. 'It isn't enough, is it?' she said flatly. 'Not without trust.'

'You want to end this?' Jean-Luc asked in quiet tones.

'When you make love to me...' She stopped, working hard to retain what little composure she had. 'You're the only one to do this to me,' she murmured. 'To make me feel so...'

'What?' Jean-Luc frowned as he looked down into her face.

'So...frightened.'

'I *frighten* you?'

'You know what I mean!' Rachel's reply was sharp.' And if you don't, then...' She shook her head slowly. 'I can't go through that again,' she whispered.

'You think *I* can?'

.'That's why, maybe, it's better...' If he loved her, wouldn't he have told her by now? she reasoned. *Wouldn't he?* But, then, he had told her he loved her once before, and what difference had that made to him? He had still walked away. 'Yes,' she replied stiltedly, 'I think we should...end this thing...now before it gets... before we both get—'

'*Hurt?*' His voice was suddenly harsh. He cursed, low and succinct and very French. 'You really haven't changed, have you?'

Rachel threw him an agonised look. 'I don't know what you mean.'

'I should have stayed in France!' He shook his head, throwing back the covers to reveal the full extent of his naked body. Muscles rippled as he reached for his clothes. 'I will go. Here!' He tossed the watch onto the bed. 'It is expensive. You will need to return it to him.'

Rachel felt sick despair flood her body. 'Jean-Luc!'

'You see how you change me?' he muttered tightly. 'How can we ever hope to—?' He didn't continue—he didn't have to. Rachel understood the way his mind was working. 'The past is important. I was a fool to imagine otherwise.' His voice shook with a hard, intense emotion. 'It alters everything.'

She forced herself to say it, to put aside any pride, to ask outright so that there would be no misunderstandings, no recriminations and might-have-beens. 'Don't you love me?'

His expression changed, but not for the better, and Rachel knew in that moment, as his mouth tightened ominously and his dark brows drew together in a frown, what the answer was going to be. 'And if I do?' His voice was rough edged, cruel, almost tortured. 'Would it honestly make any difference?' Jean-Luc's mouth twisted into a humourless smile.

'A stupid question. Six years ago...' He shook his head and she saw something that looked like pain in his eyes. 'I will leave the Grange,' he added in more businesslike tones. 'You will have no need to worry about my investment. Things will continue as they have done.'

'Why did you come back?' Rachel whispered. 'Just to make me suffer all over again?'

'Why, indeed? If I have to tell you then there really is little point in any of this. I made a mistake,' he asserted bluntly. 'Let us just leave it at that.'

'Go, then!' she told him bitterly. 'Go! If that's what

you want! You've ruined everything,' Rachel croaked, 'just by asking about Shaun. Just by thinking that I could have—! Go!' she repeated. 'I never want to see you again!'

CHAPTER ELEVEN

JEAN-LUC got into his car and drove. Very fast. It was a beautiful morning. The sun was just visible above the horizon, spilling golden rays across the dew-laden grass. Jean-Luc raced down the drive in his Mercedes, his eyes fixed on a point somewhere in the distance.

Out through the gates, a brief pause at the junction with the main road, then away with a squeal of tyres and the smell of burning rubber...

He had no idea where he was headed, no idea at all. The road, he eventually realised, had taken him to the coast. As good a place as any. He drove with increased caution along the winding road, conscious of the jagged cliffs falling away to his left and the white foam which sprayed the windscreen of the car every once in a while.

After an hour he stopped and parked on a grass verge. He stood, looking out to sea. He felt cold. Unprotected against the white spray and buffeting wind. He tried not to think of Rachel and failed miserably. It wasn't going to work—why couldn't he just admit it? Jean-Luc put his hands behind his head and gazed at the horizon. Across the channel was his home. *It wasn't going to work!* How could it, with him as jealous as hell and Rachel cold and angry and without sympathy or understanding?

He hardly knew what to do. He should leave—that's what she wanted, wasn't it?

Return to France, he told himself. Forget her. This time *really* forget her...

* * *

'I thought I might find you out here.'

Rachel looked up. She had been staring down at the lavender bush on her little patio in silent contemplation, wallowing in self-pity and allowing her thoughts to wander at will. 'Hello.'

'Something the matter?' Shaun crouched beside her. He tilted her chin with his hand. 'What on earth is it? You've been crying.'

She wiped at her damp face with the back of her hand. 'Not something I do very often.' Rachel attempted a smile, which didn't quite come off.

'It's him, isn't it?' His mild face was suddenly angry. 'I saw him at the Grange earlier, looking pretty dour.'

Rachel's heart jolted. 'What was he doing?'

'Oh, racing down the drive, kicking up gravel with that damned nice car of his, slamming the door, ignoring everybody and everything.' Shaun frowned. 'Anyway, why should you care if he's treated you so badly?'

'You don't know that he has.'

Shaun raised a brow. 'Well, hasn't he?'

Rachel shook her head, biting down on her bottom lip. 'I'm so stupid! It's never going to work out between us. I should have learnt from the past. I thought it was perfect then, and it ended. Why should it be any different now?'

'I wish I could help...' Shaun pulled a face, his expression full of sympathy. 'Come on,' he added, grabbing hold of Rachel's hand and hoisting her to her feet. 'Let's go for a walk. You look as if you're going to take root.'

'I don't want to go out.'

'Just around the orchard.' Shaun looked into Rachel's troubled face. 'It's a lovely evening, and the exercise will do you good. Besides, there's something I want to tell you.'

He opened the little wooden gate which led out into

the orchard and held out a hand towards a reluctant Rachel. Eventually she got to her feet. 'Just for a little while, then,' she murmured.

They strolled together side by side. After a moment Shaun said, 'I think you ought to go and visit Naomi again.'

'But she hasn't wanted to see me.' Rachel's voice was weary. She could hardly concentrate on anything except Jean-Luc. 'I thought it was agreed that it would be best if I stayed away?'

'Yes, I know, but I still think you should go.'

'Why? Has something happened?' Rachel frowned. 'She's doing OK, isn't she?'

'Yes. She's, well, not fine exactly, but the doctors seem to be a little more optimistic every time I speak with them. Her speech has definitely improved.' Shaun's expression was rueful. 'I can just about understand one in twenty words now.' He paused. 'She's been talking about you.'

'*Me?* I should go.' Rachel nodded to herself. 'Poor old Naomi, she must hate being like this. What did she say?'

'Oh...' Shaun shook his head. 'Only one in twenty words,' he reminded her. 'I can make out your name and that of your Aunt Clara. But it's not so much what she said to me as what she's been saying to one of the voluntary visitors.

'They set up this system, apparently, because Naomi was becoming so agitated about her inability to communicate. It takes her a long time because she has difficulty remembering the right words, but she pointed to letters on a board and, with the help of this visitor, spelled out at least some of what she's been wanting to say.'

'And?' They had reached the far end of the orchard. Cattle grazed in a meadow on the other side of the post and rail fence, and the west wing of the Grange, as well as the chapel, was clearly visible from here. Rachel stopped and turned towards Shaun, feeling a shaft of pain as she caught sight of the chapel. 'What was it?'

'I've got it written down.' Shaun delved into the pocket of his trousers. 'Here you are.' He handed her a crumpled piece of paper. 'It's not very much, and it's probably not that important, but I thought you should see it, anyway.'

Rachel unfolded the paper, torn from a lined notepad, and read aloud. '"Too young. Clara and me. Father." Does that say "was"? "Ill."' She looked up at Shaun and raised her eyebrows questioningly.

'I know. It's not exactly illuminating is it? But it seemed important to Naomi at the time. She definitely looks more relaxed now she's got that off her chest.'

'And you think this has something to do with me?' Rachel looked at the piece of paper again. 'It looks like just the usual reminiscences to me. You know Aunt Clara and Naomi have known each other for many years—they often used to regale me with stories from their past.'

Shaun lifted his shoulders. 'I don't know. The voluntary worker told me Naomi said what she thought was your name many times during her visit, but maybe she got it wrong. Forget it.' He plucked the paper from her fingers and threw it onto the grass.

'Now, would you like to tell me about why you're so upset?' he asked, looking into Rachel's red-rimmed eyes. He put his hand on her arm, preventing her from picking up the piece of paper. 'It is him, isn't it?' He cursed beneath his breath. 'I knew he was a bastard the first time I set eyes on him!'

'You still haven't forgiven him for throwing you out of the kitchen, have you?' Rachel murmured miserably. She shook her head and removed Shaun's hand from her arm. 'I don't want to talk about it,' she continued. 'There's nothing you can do.'

'You're too good for him.' Shaun gripped Rachel's shoulders, turning her to look into his face. 'Believe me,' he asserted. 'Far too good!'

'Shaun, please! I know you mean well, but platitudes aren't going to make me feel any better. I don't think anything will,' she added dully. 'Just let me go!' she added, her voice sounding anguished in the evening air. 'I just need to be on my own—'

Jean-Luc threw his clothes into the open suitcase on his bed, striding around his suite like a man possessed as he retrieved his few belongings from the room.

He had spent virtually all day on that cliff-top, oblivious of almost everything—just existing, conscious of the pain inside, trying very hard not to think.

His plane was waiting. He stood before the window, looking out at the setting sun. He could glimpse the lodge from here. He stared at the creamy stone, the latticed kitchen window and the overgrown garden, which Rachel had been so pleased with, and then quickly averted his gaze. Torturing himself was pointless. To see her once more would be even more so. Nothing had changed since this morning—she would still hate him, just as he hated himself.

He spun away, but turned back to the window almost immediately as a movement in the orchard caught his eye. Two people, glimpsed through the trees. Jean-Luc's body tensed as he watched Rachel and Shaun walking together. Already? She wanted to be with him so soon after…?

Perhaps not. Jean-Luc concentrated on Rachel's body language. He watched as she twisted from Shaun's grasp, as his hands reached out and tried to hold her again…

Afterwards, Rachel was to wonder how neither of them had been aware of Jean-Luc's arrival on the scene until it was too late.

One moment Shaun was standing in front of her, a pleading look in his eyes, the next he was being hauled away by strong, tanned hands. Rachel stared in surprised horror as Jean-Luc pinioned Shaun roughly against a nearby tree, gripping his checked shirt at his throat.

'I told you once before to stop pestering her,' he snarled. 'Are you really so stupid as to imagine I didn't mean it?'

'Jean-Luc. Please!' Rachel ran towards the two men, stepping back hastily as Shaun lunged out violently at Jean-Luc. 'Shaun, don't!' She glanced into his face and saw wild anger in his eyes. 'You'll get hurt!'

A scuffle ensued. Shaun clearly hadn't learned anything from his last encounter with Jean-Luc. He didn't possess anywhere near the agility or strength to deal with the situation in the way he so obviously wanted to. He swung a fist, and then another, cursing as Jean-Luc dodged out of reach and then kicking out madly. Jean-Luc then decided that attack was the best form of defence, rather as Shaun had done, but with a great deal more effectiveness.

Rachel crouched beside Shaun as he sat up, holding a tissue against his bloody nose. He was breathing hard, looking pained and defeated. She turned and glared up at Jean-Luc, who was standing a few feet away, staring down at them both. 'Animal!' she yelled. 'What did you have to do that for? He was just talking to me!'

Jean-Luc's eyes darkened at the harshness of her words. Rachel saw that he was breathing hard and that there was a graze on the side of his head where Shaun's fist had connected. 'It did not look that way from the Grange,' he asserted.

'You were spying on us?'

'*Spying?*' She saw the anger in his eyes. 'I saw you together.' His mouth tightened. 'He had his hands on you.'

'And if he did? What has that to do with you?' Rachel replied croakily. A part of her wanted to get up and go to him, to thank him for defending her honour—even if he had got it all wrong—but she glanced back at Shaun, breathing deeply, using the time to compose herself, to convince herself that hostility was the best barrier for holding back the pain.

'Shaun and I are friends!' she told him, her blue eyes narrowed and cold. 'He cares about me. And what makes you think I want you interfering, anyway? I don't! Never!' Her voice trembled and she had to take another deep breath. 'Never again!' She looked at Shaun's bloody nose. 'How could you be so hateful?'

'I thought...I thought you needed me. It seems I was wrong.' Jean-Luc's voice, after sufficient composure had kicked in, was cold, empty of expression. 'Forgive me.' His gaze shifted from Rachel's face. The two men looked at each other. 'I apologise,' he announced quietly. 'It seems that one way or another,' he murmured, and his message was clear as he looked at Rachel again, 'I am destined to make a great many mistakes.'

'Perhaps you are,' she said crisply. She couldn't weaken now, even though she wanted to—so much. 'Believe me,' she murmured, her eyes glistening with tears. 'I never wanted things to end up this way.'

'And last time?' he asked roughly. His eyes held hers. 'What about then?'

'*Last time?*' Rachel could hardly think straight, her emotions were in such turmoil. She made a huge effort to collect her wits. 'What do you mean?'

'A sudden memory loss?' He slanted her a look of sardonic enquiry. 'It's easier to pretend it didn't happen when you've acted badly, isn't it?'

'I…' Rachel shook her head. 'I don't know what you're talking about,' she murmured. '*Why?*' she whispered. 'Why do you have to be so cruel?'

'I am the one who is cruel?' A look of amazement flashed across Jean-Luc's handsome face. He uttered a curse under his breath, low and volatile and very French.

'I do not believe this!' he exclaimed. 'You talk to me about being cruel?' He shook his head, and Rachel saw a sudden flash of pain in his eyes, a look which so mirrored her own feelings that she wanted to cry. He turned away from them both. 'I must go!' It was a fervent thought, voiced aloud, rather than a cool statement of fact.

'Yes, do us all a favour—get the hell out!' Shaun's belligerent tone made Rachel wince. She saw the restraint Jean-Luc had to exert to keep cool.

'Shaun, shut up!' Rachel got to her feet. 'I'm sorry,' she murmured.

Jean-Luc raised a dark brow. 'For your friend? Don't be.' He began to move away, but stooped suddenly and picked up something from the grass. 'Yours?' he queried. 'A love note, perhaps?' He glanced down at the lined paper. Rachel watched as a frown settled itself on his forehead. 'What is this?'

'Just…something Naomi wanted to say,' Rachel murmured. 'She isn't making much sense at the moment, as you can see.'

'It seems she, too, is obsessed with our past,' he commented as he handed the note back. 'Not unusual, perhaps, given the fact that she so often tried to interfere.'

'*Our* past?' Rachel read the words again. 'What makes you say that? This isn't about us.'

'Isn't it?'

'No, it's about Naomi and Aunt Clara when they were young. They grew up together. Naomi came here to serve as a young girl back in the nineteen-thirties.'

'And this part?' Jean-Luc pointed to the note, reading aloud, '"Father was ill." That doesn't mean anything to you?' There was a hint of scorn in his voice.

'No.' Puzzled, Rachel looked up into Jean-Luc's face. 'Why—should it?'

'You have a conveniently short memory.' His voice was clipped. 'No matter, if that is the way you want to play it.'

He began to walk away and had moved several metres before Rachel decided to go after him. 'I don't know what you're talking about!' she asserted angrily, taking hold of his arm. 'I really don't!' she said, dropping her hand because to touch him was the kind of torturous agony she didn't need right now—not on top of everything else. 'Why don't you just explain it all to me, instead of flouncing off?'

A spark of unexpected humour twisted Jean-Luc's mouth. Rachel's heart leapt in her chest. '*Flounce*?' he queried.

'You know what I mean,' she replied irritably. 'Stop looking so…so critical, and tell me!' she urged.

'That my father was ill?' He lifted broad shoulders in a shrug. 'There, it is done.'

'Your father?' Rachel expression was blank. 'When?'

'Your memory is still playing tricks?' Jean-Luc did not look impressed. 'Perhaps it has something to do with guilt?'

'Guilt?' Rachel's face at once became animated. 'Now I *really* don't know what you are talking about!' she said. 'Why should I feel guilty?'

'Did our relationship really mean so little to you?' Jean-Luc demanded. 'Did *I*?'

He began to walk away again—long strides which covered the ground swiftly so that Rachel had to almost run to keep up with him. She heard Shaun's voice calling to her with dire warnings and advice about leaving well alone, but she ignored it.

'Jean-Luc, please!' She stepped in front of him, halting his progress.

He stopped, looking down at her with such a tortured, unhappy expression that she gasped and reached out towards him in such a way as to indicate that she could see his pain. 'You have no idea,' he assured her quietly, 'of how I feel inside.'

Rachel swallowed. 'No...' she whispered, as she looked into his eyes, 'maybe I don't...'

'I thought we'd spend the rest of our lives together,' he continued in husky tones. 'I thought that was what you wanted.'

'I did!' Rachel's reply conveyed all her emotion. 'I do,' she added softly.

He seemed hardly to hear her as he continued to speak. 'When I left to return to France I had no idea how serious the situation was, how long I'd have to stay away. I was worried, sure, but secure in the knowledge that what we shared together would stand any amount of disruption or upheaval.' His dark eyes surveyed her face with a frown. 'I thought our love was strong,' he murmured. 'I thought it would stand the test of time.'

'Your father was ill?'

'I've already told you—'

'And that is why you went away—why you left so suddenly?'

He looked at her quizzically. 'Of course.'

Rachel's blonde head shook. 'No,' she asserted, 'this doesn't make sense. You left a letter, telling me...' Her voice trembled, and she stopped to take a deep breath, before continuing, 'Telling me that...that you didn't want to see me again, that you had decided our relationship was becoming too restrained, that you felt hemmed-in, trapped. That you'd enjoyed what we'd shared but...but that there was a whole world out there, waiting for you—'

'You believe that I could have ever written such a note?' The incredulity in Jean-Luc's voice was strong.

'I...I didn't want to believe it,' Rachel began, 'but...' She shook her head, her expression a confusion of conflicting emotions. *'You didn't write to me?'* she asked breathlessly.

'I wrote.' Compared to the fragility of Rachel's tones, Jean-Luc's voice was strong and sure. 'Yes. But to tell you that my father was ill and that I had to go to him— that I didn't know how long I would be away.' His dark eyes narrowed. 'Are you telling me now that you never saw my letter?'

Rachel pressed a trembling hand to her mouth, her blue eyes glistening with tears. This was all so...so wonderful and at the same time so dreadful. 'No...at least...' She shook her head. 'You never wanted to break up with me?' she whispered. 'You were always going to return?'

'I did return. About ten days later. I had tried calling and writing but you were never there, and when you didn't answer any of my letters—'

'I couldn't bear staying here without you,' Rachel whispered. 'I returned early from my friend's wedding— you remember I was due to stay a couple of nights?'

'I remember.'

'When I came home and read what you had written...' She could hardly speak, her throat was so choked with unshed tears. 'I waited, hoping it was all just...well, that you would change your mind. I wanted to contact you, but didn't know how or where—'

'I wrote with my family's address,' Jean-Luc interposed. 'I waited for you to call—'

'But I didn't get your letter!' Rachel responded fervently. 'I didn't! Not any of them. I really thought you didn't want to see me any more, that I was just a—'

'What?' Jean-Luc's eyes pierced hers. 'A holiday romance?' he suggested, with obvious disdain. 'You thought that?'

'Yes...I suppose I did...' Rachel struggled to continue. 'Aunt Clara was kind, sympathetic. She suggested that I visit some distant relatives we have in America—' Rachel stopped suddenly and bowed her head as the full implications of what she was saying sank in. 'It was her, wasn't it?' she whispered. 'She did this to us.'

'Who else?' Jean-Luc's expression was tense.

'Naomi?' Rachel thought back, knowing that what she said was the truth. 'Yes.' She nodded slowly as she thought it all through. 'They were close. Naomi would have done anything for Aunt Clara—'

'Even lie and manipulate.' Jean-Luc nodded slowly in agreement.

'I can't believe that either of them could do this!' Rachel's voice was stronger now as disbelief faded and anger took hold. 'How could they? I knew Aunt Clara didn't particularly approve of our relationship, but—'

'You were young, sweet.' Jean-Luc shook his head. 'It's I who should have realised. I received a letter from you.' His eyes took in Rachel's shocked expression. His jaw clenched. 'At least, I thought I did. You never wrote?' Rachel shook her head. He ran a hand through his thick, dark hair. 'It was convincing...' He released a tense breath. 'You were very young. I knew that. Even while I was falling in love with you I kept reminding myself, telling myself, that just because I wanted this so very badly—wanted you—that our situation could change, that you might change—'

'Never!' Rachel was adamant. 'Never,' she repeated. 'Both of them were so clever,' she whispered, thinking back, 'so careful to play it exactly right. I never suspected—not for a moment.'

'It crossed my mind that your aunt might have some

involvement,' Jean-Luc admitted, 'but only in so far as you might have finally taken her advice and decided to end our relationship. I really didn't believe that another human being could go to such lengths, could be so—'

'Manipulative? Cruel?' Rachel's voice trembled. 'I was so...miserable,' she told him. 'I felt battered...weak. I couldn't think straight for months afterwards. Oh, Jean-Luc!' Tears spilled over at last and ran down Rachel's cheeks. 'What have they done to us?'

He pulled her into his arms and held her close. Rachel clung to him, her eyes tightly shut, and tried not to think about the years of misery she had endured—they had both endured—unnecessarily.

'Nothing that cannot be put right,' he murmured huskily. 'You must know...' His voice was unsteady as he spoke, deep, sensual, full of emotion. Was this really happening? he wondered. 'How much I still love you. All those arguments, those harsh words... I've been the biggest kind of fool.' He drew back and looked down into her face. 'Forgive me,' he whispered, 'for ever doubting you.'

'There is nothing to forgive.' Rachel's voice was soft. 'You love me, and I love you—truly—that's all that matters.'

'*Ma chérie.*' Jean-Luc lowered his head then and covered her mouth with his in a kiss that was sensuous and tender—that told her better than words ever could just how much she meant to him. 'No more mistakes,' he asserted forcibly, looking deep into her eyes. 'No more misunderstandings.'

Rachel kissed his mouth. 'We've had enough to last a lifetime,' she whispered.

'A lifetime, yes...' His voice was husky. 'I wish to ask you something,' he murmured softly, his mouth against hers, his lips, like his voice, teasing with obvious pleasure.

'Ask me what?' Rachel's body was trembling with desire. She wanted him so much it almost hurt.

'To marry me.' His kiss was deep and rich with love. 'We were meant for each other.'

'Oh, Jean-Luc! Yes! *Yes!*' Rachel's blue eyes glittered with tears. 'To be your wife would be the most wonderful thing in the world! I love you,' she said happily. 'For ever and always.'

'Sounds good,' Jean-Luc replied. His smile was warm and sensuous. 'My perfect partner,' he murmured huskily, looking deep into Rachel's glistening eyes. 'For eternity…'

EPILOGUE

THE crisp smell of autumn filled the air. Rachel wandered through the orchard, carefully stepping along the freshly mown pathway. The leaves were changing colour, hints of burnished gold and reds mixing with the last remaining apples which still clung to the branches overhead.

Her dress was of ivory satin, long and slim-fitting, the bodice encrusted with tiny seed pearls. She wore flowers in her hair and carried long stems of pale pink roses.

It was a special walk from the grounds of the Grange to the tiny private chapel. Rachel had wanted to do it this way, to take her vows here—a fitting way of closing one chapter of her life and opening another.

She took her time, and focused on the peace and solitude of the moment, walking alone, each step slow and measured, bringing her nearer to the love of her life.

The grounds looked lovely in the morning sunlight. It was early. There was no one around in this deliberately neglected part of the grounds. Peaceful. Perfect.

Jean-Luc stood outside the small stone chapel, waiting for her. Inside were a few carefully chosen guests—Jean-Luc's family, including a fully recovered Maria, who was, indeed, as beautiful as Rachel had imagined, and Naomi, wheelchair-bound but stronger and happier now that the weight of guilt had been removed from her shoulders.

Rachel smiled as she approached. She was hardly able to believe that this wonderful event was about to take place.

Jean-Luc looked magnificent in his dark suit, so tall

and handsome, his dark eyes so full of love, as he held out his hands toward her.

'I love you,' he whispered, looking deep into her eyes.

'I love you, too,' Rachel replied softly.

He kissed her tenderly. 'Thank you.'

Rachel's eyes glistened. 'For what?'

'For waiting, for being patient—for wanting to be my wife.'

'We nearly didn't make it.'

'I know.' Jean-Luc's eyes smouldered as he looked down into her face. 'If I ever lose you again...!'

'Shh!' Rachel placed a finger to his lips. 'Our love is strong,' she told him. 'It will endure.'

She glanced toward the open chapel door, catching a glimpse of the waiting vicar. 'Everyone ready?'

'Yes.'

'Even Naomi?'

'Even her.'

Rachel kissed his mouth. 'You've done a very honourable thing,' she murmured, 'agreeing to pay for her future care. I love you for it—have I told you that?'

Jean-Luc's mouth twisted humourously. 'Once or twice, but you can tell me again. I'll never get tired of hearing you say it.'

'Shall we go inside?'

A smile tugged at the corners of Jean-Luc's mouth. 'I think that's a very good idea,' he said.

The ceremony was simple and very moving. Afterwards they ran along the rear drive to a waiting limousine, festooned with ribbons. Emile, the chauffeur, opened the car door, smiling at them both.

'Where to, Madame Manoire?' Jean-Luc enquired teasingly.

'Anywhere!' Rachel replied, laughing, as she threw her roses into the air. 'It doesn't matter, as long as I'm with you.'

MARGOT DALTON

second thoughts

To Detective Jackie Kaminsky it seemed like a routine
burglary, until she took a second look at the
evidence... The intruder knew his way around
Maribel Lewis's home—yet took nothing.
He *seems* to know Maribel's deepest secret—
and wants payment in blood.

A spellbinding new Kaminsky mystery.

1-55166-421-6
**AVAILABLE IN PAPERBACK
FROM OCTOBER, 1998**

Jennifer
BLAKE

KANE

Down in Louisiana, family comes first.
That's the rule the Benedicts live by.
So when a beautiful redhead starts paying a little
too much attention to Kane Benedict's grandfather,
Kane decides to find out what her *real* motives are.

*"Blake's style is as steamy as a still July night...as overwhelming
hot as Cajun spice."*

—Chicago Times

MIRA®

1-55166-429-1
AVAILABLE IN PAPERBACK
FROM OCTOBER, 1998

EMILIE RICHARDS

THE WAY BACK HOME

As a teenager, Anna Fitzgerald fled an impossible
situation, only to discover that life on the streets was
worse. But she had survived. Now, as a woman,
she lived with the constant threat that the secrets of
her past would eventually destroy her new life.

1-55166-399-6
AVAILABLE IN PAPERBACK
FROM SEPTEMBER, 1998

JASMINE CRESSWELL

THE DAUGHTER

Maggie Slade's been on the run for seven years now.
Seven years of living without a life or a future because
she's a woman with a past. And then she meets Sean
McLeod. Maggie has two choices. She can either run,
or learn to trust again and prove her innocence.

"Romantic suspense at its finest."

—Affaire de Coeur

1-55166-425-9
AVAILABLE IN PAPERBACK
FROM SEPTEMBER, 1998

CHRISTIANE
HEGGAN

SUSPICION

Kate Logan's gut instincts told her that neither of her
clients was guilty of murder, and homicide detective
Mitch Calhoon wanted to help her prove it. What neither suspected was how dangerous the truth would be.

*"Christiane Heggan delivers a tale that will leave you
breathless."*

—Literary Times

1-55166-305-8
AVAILABLE IN PAPERBACK
FROM SEPTEMBER, 1998

DEBBIE MACOMBER

Married in Montana

Needing a safe place for her sons to grow up, Molly
Cogan decided it was time to return home.
Home to Sweetgrass Montana.
Home to her grandfather's ranch.

*"Debbie Macomber's name on a book is a guarantee
of delightful, warm-hearted romance."*
—Jayne Ann Krentz

1-55166-400-3
AVAILABLE IN PAPERBACK
FROM AUGUST, 1998